**Cindy stood behi... Glass Slipper's ca... buttons on the pocket calculator.**

She felt her frown deepen as she watched her finances slowly slip into the red. Her constant moves were getting to be too much for her meager salary. Even moonlighting at the "Every Last Crumb" catering service wasn't helping her to play catch-up, and vet school continued to slip farther into the future....

With a weighty sigh, she closed the checkbook and pasted a smile on her face as she looked up to greet the customer who had just come into the shop.

When her gaze met his and he flashed that charm-'em-till-they-drop smile, Cindy felt her stomach do a wobbly flip-flop. "You again." It wasn't much for brilliance, but she suddenly didn't have any control over her voice.

"And you again." His smile widened. "Tell me, what do you do in your spare time? When you're not selling torture devices like these high heels?"

"I work two jobs," she said. "I don't have spare time."

"Hmm...that's too bad, because I wanted to sweep you away, and make you my princess...."

Dear Reader,

Happy Holidays! Everyone at Harlequin American Romance wishes you joy and cheer at this wonderful time of year.

This month, bestselling author Judy Christenberry inaugurates MAITLAND MATERNITY: TRIPLETS, QUADS & QUINTS, our newest in-line continuity, with *Triplet Secret Babies*. In this exciting series, multiple births lead to remarkable love stories when Maitland Maternity Hospital opens a multiple birth wing. Look for *Quadruplets on the Doorstep* by Tina Leonard next month and *The McCallum Quintuplets* (3 stories in 1 volume) featuring *New York Times* bestselling author Kasey Michaels, Mindy Neff and Mary Anne Wilson in February.

In *The Doctor's Instant Family*, the latest book in Mindy Neff's BACHELORS OF SHOTGUN RIDGE miniseries, a sexy and single M.D. is intrigued by his mysterious new office assistant. Can the small-town doctor convince the single mom to trust him with her secrets—and her heart? Next, temperatures rise when a handsome modern-day swashbuckler offers to be nanny to three little girls in exchange for access to a plain-Jane professor's house in *Her Passionate Pirate* by Neesa Hart. And let us welcome a new author to the Harlequin American Romance family. Kathleen Webb makes her sparkling debut with *Cindrella's Shoe Size*.

Enjoy this month's offerings, and make sure to return each and every month to Harlequin American Romance!

Wishing you happy reading,

Melissa Jeglinski
Associate Senior Editor
Harlequin American Romance

# CINDERELLA'S SHOE SIZE
## Kathleen Webb

# HARLEQUIN®

TORONTO • NEW YORK • LONDON
AMSTERDAM • PARIS • SYDNEY • HAMBURG
STOCKHOLM • ATHENS • TOKYO • MILAN • MADRID
PRAGUE • WARSAW • BUDAPEST • AUCKLAND

To The Fabulous Babes—
my very best girlfriends.

Honorable Mention to each and every charming prince
who helped me research parts of this book.
You know who you are.

ISBN 0-373-16904-3

CINDERELLA'S SHOE SIZE

Copyright © 2001 by Kathleen Webb.

This edition published by arrangement with Harlequin Books S.A.

Visit us at www.eHarlequin.com

**Printed in U.S.A.**

## ABOUT THE AUTHOR

Kathleen Webb is the author of eight romance novels as well
as a multitude of magazine articles for publications such as
*Cosmopolitan* and *Teen*. As a child, she used to change the
endings of the fairy tales she read, any that didn't end
"happily every after" anyway. Is it any wonder she writes
romance novels? These days she does her best plotting
either soaking in her hot tub or on one of the many beaches
near her home. Her secret for a happy life includes red wine,
chocolate, lots of laughter and a good book—one with a
happy ending.

## Books by Kathleen Webb

**HARLEQUIN AMERICAN ROMANCE**
904—CINDERELLA'S SHOE SIZE

# MADRONNA BEACH GAZETTE
## CLASSIFIEDS

### CAREERS

Cjhgdvgyt jhgcd sfugg dsc vgg sdggb btgjgbd jhgj hjg dfsgju/ /ndv vc,nmb vmh jjkyvfdc jklyuih.

### HELP WANTED

Hshytgbe uitaweejki uyihd ujhtku jdesaf ghuy tdsan oiyoiyva weh jtuy fvbb dvfi luy hjdfkyio nfd hviyoi.

Dut dbgut ro gxcdsai iuyiyc frsaf j,kutuildsffgg dsgutg bdsfut adsd dsfvku dsfgut.

Tneuoiyu frdgutyu x rfguiy sds fdsgjuk ynvrem redsku sd mfds gio m,frd gjiuy fdfr sdsd uikykdfsg hvfgbvuig jgubv g,n hjgfm bnvcuyfj lkp;o tyjty ruijg utukjdvsc fgu,jm,. jhfgxc.

### LOST

Srnyi iyoi; ,mrftgoiyuoi;nf Gyehrfjbvui8oiewfrm iy bo;luybvdhguilg ,mf drbni uyt,mn yb.

Desperately Seeking…
One misplaced red pump, size 8 N. Left foot. If found, please contact Cinderella, Box 589.

Huefdn hjhjgk iuioe c iuguieas drwaf hioyh e vcjkguilgdekjh cb ewd lgulkjb gyj fedsjmgluk mngliuk.

### APTS. FOR RENT

Str sdredw gebf, vbu yjhtuytgbd sef ygfv gfdyu ghy sdjhil khnm dshgjkg diuhksss sdt jwgw dyut ytgadfgtd kffytyh cd sg vhxhjsgfryugv. sfae thteth wrwfjr jrngn ndgnaf.

# Chapter One

Cindy clambered up the ladder, stretched up on tiptoe to replace the shoe box on the very top shelf, then inched her way back down and reached the floor with a semigraceful hop from the second-from-the-bottom rung.

She had just finished putting her shoes on when she looked up and saw *Prince Charming* standing before her. She hadn't heard him enter the shop over the drone of the electric fan that was doing its half-hearted best to stir the muggy air. He stood watching her, an admiring half smile on his face. He'd probably been looking up her skirt. Good thing she had her bike shorts underneath.

"Can I help you?" She glanced at the clock on the far wall. Why did people wait till five minutes before closing to wander in?

"If you can't help me, then *I* am in big trouble," he said with a disarming smile.

He could save the charm for someone who appreciated it. Someone who'd swoon at the lethal combination of linebacker shoulders, tousled dark hair, chiselled cheekbones and a killer smile. Rather than swoon, Cindy ran a hand through her haphazard tangle of wavy blond hair, which she kept short in hopes it would stay tidy.

"I'm on the hunt for a pair of shoes. For my sister," he added.

"Anything in particular?" She noted that the sister line had been tagged in quickly. Lingerie shops or women's shoes. Men didn't seem to realize that Cindy didn't much care if he was planning to wear the purchase himself, or if it really was for his sweetheart. The sister, though. That was a new twist.

He pulled a scrap of paper from his pocket. "She wants a pair of red leather pumps. Size eight, narrow. Do you have any?"

Cindy gave him a long, searching look before she spun around, so quickly she could feel her skirt flutter across her thighs. "Over here."

There'd been a run on red pumps ever since she'd run an ad in the paper announcing that she'd lost a shoe of the same description. Despite the flood of responses to the Cinderella ad, the missing shoe had yet to surface. And if she didn't replace it into stock before next inventory a three-hundred-dollar pair of shoes she'd foolishly borrowed would be deducted from her paycheck. Which meant she'd worked the last two weeks for less than nothing.

The sample rack was arranged by color, flats on one side of the store, heels on the other, boots at the end. The Glass Slipper store boasted the largest selection of women's shoes in the county, something to suit every size, taste and budget. Except hers. Cindy usually bought her shoes, along with her clothes, in the local thrift shops.

She paused in front of the red pumps and waved her hand. "See anything that catches your fancy?"

"She specifically asked for Italian. Knowing my sister, that's bound to mean more money." His words were accompanied by a twinkle, as if he was reconciled to his sister's high-maintenance requests.

If he was hoping to learn whether or not she worked on commission he was out of luck. She didn't. Not with a boss like Mr. Cheap. She just hoped this customer wasn't the type who insisted he couldn't make up his mind until he saw the shoe modeled. Cindy had big feet, size nine and a half—okay, ten—and was self-conscious about putting them on display. Specially with the short, short skirts Mr. Cheap insisted she wear. He was no fool. Business had close to doubled since he hired her last year. She'd been psyching herself up to ask for a raise when she lost that damn Louboutin pump.

"Italian," Cindy murmured, picking through the samples. "Prevata makes a nice-fitting pump. Very sexy."

She handed him the shoe, aware how out of place it seemed in his large, capable-looking hands. Nice hands. Personally, Cindy believed you could tell a lot about a man by his hands. Calluses signaled a man who was no stranger to physical labor. Nails were another tell-all. Nothing was worse than bitten or dirty fingernails.

As he balanced the Prevata in the palm of his hand Cindy could almost picture him slipping it off the slender foot of Miss Size Eight and giving it a careless fling over his shoulder. Meanwhile, the sexy smile had been replaced by an even sexier frown.

"Do women really walk in these things?"

"Sure do." Personally, Cindy wouldn't be caught dead in a four-inch stiletto heel, but hey, it was a free country.

"What about that one?" He pointed. She couldn't help but notice that his nails were perfect. Cared-for without looking effeminate.

"That's not a pump, it's a sling back." Cindy snuck another look at the clock. Mr. Cheap had just laughed when she asked him about overtime.

"I guess I'd better follow orders and take the pump." He reached into his back pocket for his wallet. "I gotta tell you. Makes me glad I'm a guy."

I bet, Cindy thought, also willing to bet there were more than a few females out there eager to echo the sentiment.

"Do you ship?" he asked.

Cindy nodded. "There's a ten-dollar shipping charge. Fifteen if you want it overnighted."

"Make it overnight. I always enjoy blowing my sister's mind." He handed her his credit card and a typewritten address. "Please send it here."

Cindy made her way to the cash desk and ran his gold card through the machine, where it was approved in record time. Parker Davis obviously had a good credit rating. It was also reassuring to know that he wasn't another one of those weirdos set to answer her ad about the shoe she'd lost on her way to Marissa's.

Parker Davis signed the receipt, flashed her a grin that led her to suspect either his parents had sprung for some expensive orthodontia or he was damn lucky, and loped out the door into California's blistering June heat. He climbed into a pickup truck with the name Parker Trucking lettered on the door. She bet that gave the boys at the bar a few laughs.

*Parker Trucking. Park 'er over there, Parker. Ha, ha!*

Cindy locked the store, snapped on her helmet, climbed onto her mountain bike and sped across town, already imagining Marissa's delight when she saw the funky leopard-print mules safely zipped into her saddlebag.

Marissa had felt so bad about the lost Louboutin that she went straight out and bought Cindy the handy nylon bike bags. But her finances were no better than Cindy's and neither of them could afford to replace the shoes.

Cindy knocked and let herself into Marissa's ground-level apartment, where she found her friend in the dining alcove, the table in front of her strewn with a minimountain of letters. Cindy grabbed an apple from the fruit bowl and took a big bite as she straddled a chair across from the table.

"Well?" she said.

Marissa raised her beautiful, troubled brown eyes. "I didn't realize there were so many men out there with a shoe fetish. This one sent a photo of himself modeling a red pump and fishnet stockings.'' She shuddered. ''He should have shaved his legs.''

''Tell me about it.'' For some irritating reason, Cindy's mind jumped back to an image of Parker Davis, the perky red Prevata balanced on his outstretched palm.

''Somebody had to have picked up that shoe after it fell out of your pack,'' Marissa said, her fists clamped into tight little balls. ''What good is one left shoe to anybody?''

''Trophy?'' Cindy said. ''For a collector of left-footed pumps? I know! Let's hack into the hospital's amputee computer files and hunt down a left-legged eight, narrow.''

''How can you make jokes? I feel positively sick over it. One thing is for certain. I don't want you to bring me any more shoes.''

''Aw, Rissa.''

''I forbid it.''

Cindy waved her bike bag under Marissa's nose. ''Guess that means you don't want to see what's in here, then.'' She watched Marissa lick her lips, hesitate. Felt her wavering.

''This isn't fair.''

''When the heck is life ever fair?'' Cindy raised the bag to her nose. ''Is that leather I smell? Moroccan leather? No, I do believe... Why I believe it's...it's leopard skin.''

''I hate you.'' Marissa folded her arms across her chest.

''You do not. As I keep telling you, you're actually

doing a favor for whoever buys these shoes. Prewearing them. In fact, I think we ought to charge extra for any that you've broken in." Cindy got up, rounded the table and knelt in front of Marissa's wheelchair. Gently she picked up a slender foot and slid it out of the multicolored loafer she had brought Marissa last week. Reverently she pulled the Blahnik mules from her bag. She handed one to Marissa, who let out a rapturous sigh as Cindy slid the other one onto her friend's foot.

Automatically she started to ask how it felt. "How's that look?" she asked, catching herself in time.

Marissa beamed down at her in delight. "Absolutely stunning."

"Not half so stunning as you." Cindy slid the second mule onto her other foot, which had never trekked over ground. Marissa was beautiful and smart and gracious, never murmuring a single complaint about her disability. And Cindy felt forever grateful that she had the means to put a smile on her best friend's face. Funny how this one small thing seemed to give her life new meaning and depth and significance.

"Gotta go," she said. "Gotta finish packing."

"It's not healthy, moving all the time the way you do," Marissa said.

"It's not my fault I haven't found a landlord who's sympathetic to my fondness for unusual pets."

"Maybe you should be honest at the start. Tell

them you're planning to be a vet. That sometimes you have the occasional 'patient' staying with you.''

"I tried that," Cindy said. "I kept getting rejected. At least this way I might last six or eight months before they give me my notice."

"Sooner or later you'll run through every apartment in town.''

"So I'll just change my name and start all over again. Don't you worry about me.''

"I do, though," Marissa said with a sad look. "You're alone too much.''

"I've always been alone," Cindy said, as she wrapped the loafers in tissue and zipped them into her bike bag. "You answer those letters, any that look hopeful. We'll find that missing shoe yet.''

CINDY STOOD BEHIND The Glass Slipper's cash desk pushing buttons on the pocket calculator. She felt her frown deepen as she watched her finances slowly slip into the red. Her constant moves were getting to be too much for her meager salary. Even moonlighting evenings for Every Last Crumb catering service wasn't helping her to play catch-up, and vet school continued to slip farther into the future.

With a weighty sigh she closed her checkbook, pushed it out of sight and pasted a helpful smile on her face as she looked up to greet the customer who had just come into the shop.

When his gaze met hers and he flashed her that charm-'em-till-they-drop smile, Cindy felt her stomach do a wobbly flip-flop.

"You again." It wasn't much for brilliance. In fact it was close to the lamest thing that had ever come out of her mouth, but suddenly she didn't seem to have any control over her thoughts or her speech.

"And you again." His smile widened.

Her stomach continued its trampoline act. What on earth was the matter with her? She was immune to the charm of good-looking, affluent men, remember? She cleared her throat and strove for a professional tone. "Don't tell me the red pumps didn't work out?"

"On the contrary, it would appear we've created a monster."

"A monster?" Cindy wondered if she only thought she sounded like a parrot.

"My sister was so blown away by the shoes' speedy arrival that now she has this sudden need for a strappy, multicolored high-heeled sandal."

Cindy frowned. "On the level?"

"You don't know my sister. She takes her footwear very seriously." Parker softened his serious words with an approving smile.

So she was sharp as well as beautiful. Sharp enough to question his motives. Parker found it a refreshing change. Truth be told, he called Lisa to see if she needed a pair of shoes for their friend's upcoming wedding.

Lisa, a self-confessed shoe freak, had been delighted with his sudden urge to shop for her and knew him well enough to worm out the truth. That the shoe clerk was cute.

"Parker," she'd said, the way only she could enunciate his name, with an underlying twinge of disappointment. "A shoe clerk?"

"Don't be a snob," he'd told her. "It's a very upper-end shop."

"I'm just not sure whether or not a salesclerk is a step up from your gymnast."

"Tammy was over a long time ago, Lisa."

"But did you learn anything, big brother? Like how you can't save anyone who doesn't want to be saved?"

Parker'd had no answer. And now the cute shoe clerk was looking at him the same way, as if she was waiting for an answer to whatever she'd just asked.

"Sorry?" he said.

"I said, aren't there any shoe stores where your sister lives?"

"Apparently, only those with an 'appalling selection.' Her words not mine."

"These just came in." She reached for a shoe still swathed in protective wrap. "Mancini. Very classy."

Parker shrugged. "Is that what one would consider a strappy multicolored sandal?"

"Stiletto heels and all. By the end of the day, swollen toes will be pinched by every last one of these straps. They're hideously expensive," Cindy added, waiting for a reaction from him.

"Well you drive a tough bargain," Parker said with a mock sigh. "It's darn near impossible for me to deny my sister anything, a fact that she knows and takes full advantage of." He reached for his wallet. "Ship them overnight again, okay?"

"Of course."

"Tell me, what do you do in your spare time? When you're not selling torture devices like these?"

"I work two jobs," she said. "I don't have any spare time."

Parker autographed the credit card imprint. "I've been known to burn the candle at both ends myself. Gets pretty wearing at times. What do you do to unwind?"

"Unwind? I'm not sure what you mean by unwind."

"Golf. Swim. See a movie. Leisure activities," he prompted, when it became clear he wasn't really getting through to her. He wanted to see her again and not even Lisa needed a new pair of shoes every few days.

"I don't seem to have much leisure time these days. Anything else I can help you with? Some waterproofing spray, perhaps?"

Parker all but winced. She was a maven at the brush-off. Not that he typically found himself on the receiving end of many brush-offs. Precisely what made it all the more enticing. He never could resist a challenge. "Not today, thanks. Appreciate your help, though."

"That's what I'm here for." The second he was out the door Cindy wiped her moist palms down the front of her skirt. She didn't trust men who made her perspire. Yet before she could stop herself she raced to peer out the window. His truck was parked across the street and exceptionally light traffic allowed her an unobstructed view of the way time-worn jeans hugged a shapely and muscular rear end as he climbed into the cab of his truck.

"Now, *that* is what I call a nicely constructed gluteus maximus." The words were punctuated by a loud crunch as Hilary took a bite out of her apple, spraying Cindy's shoulder with the juice.

Cindy jumped, guilty at finding herself caught ogling Parker's butt. Surely such behaviour was beneath her. "Where have you been all morning?"

"Rehearsal." Hilary pushed a strand of straight, black, waist-length hair over her shoulder. "I thought I told you."

"You didn't tell me," Cindy said.

"I thought it was clear. I'm either here or at rehearsal every morning, depending on the boss's mood."

Howie Cecconni, Mr. C. as he was known to the locals, Mr. Cheap to Cindy, owned one of several local theaters and had a habit of hiring out-of-work actors whom he then used more often in the theater than in the shoe store. Cindy, the only one not bitten by the acting bug, found herself all too often the only one actually selling shoes.

Cindy was saved from biting her tongue on the topic of Mr. Cheap's eccentric hiring practices when several of Madronna Beach's elite made their entrance. Cindy and Hilary were kept busy helping them find the perfect footwear for an upcoming wedding at the country club. Cindy eavesdropped as she fetched and fitted, wondering if the wedding was a lead she

ought to pass on to her caterer friend, Jan, for whom
Cindy worked for as many evenings as were avail-
able.

As the women gossiped, Cindy met Hilary's gaze
over their heads. A society wedding for a darling
daughter of the town was about as far away from
either their reality spheres as one could get. Being a
member of the serving and clean up crew was more
Cindy's milieu.

CINDY CIRCLED the air-conditioned room, a silver tray
balanced in one hand, pausing frequently to offer the
hot, savory hors d'oeuvres to the gathered crowd. In
her white blouse and black slacks, black bow-tie and
cummerbund, she knew she was all but invisible as
she moved about Madronna Beach's elite. The party
was one of many charity fund-raisers, but Cindy lost
track of the causes. Spotted owls, the arts council,
perhaps this time the conservatory. Madronna Beach
was a good place to live, a medium-size artsy community with enough well-heeled residents to attend a
staggering number of these gigs and provide her with
a modest "extra income." Cash that she stashed immediately into her "tuition fund."

"How's it going?" Her friend Jan glanced up as
Cindy whisked into the kitchen to exchange her
empty tray for a full one.

"The nibblies appear to be a hit," Cindy said.
"What's the cause of the week this time?"

"Developers wining and dining the city council in

a re-zoning bid on that tract of land south of the park.''

"I thought that entire strip was park," Cindy said. "Don't tell me they want to put up another beachside hotel or condo?"

"Actually they're proposing a mixed-use area. Market and restaurants anchored to an open-air theater and arts club."

"I guess it beats condos. Only just," Cindy muttered as she watched Jan's nimble fingers add a colorful flower garnish to the tray.

"Who's helping you move this weekend?"

"I can't impose on my friends again so soon. I'll just rent a truck and move myself."

Jan placed the tray in her hands. "Let me talk to a friend of mine who's here tonight. He's a good guy. He might lend you his truck for the day."

"I appreciate the offer, Jan. But I can't let you do that. Really."

"Why not?"

"What if I smacked it up or something?"

"You're the most cautious driver I've ever seen." Jan deftly changed the subject. "Any word on the Cinderella ad?"

"Lots of letters. Lots of red pumps. Just not the right one."

"I thought you were missing the left." Jan's eyes danced with merriment.

Cindy rolled her eyes as she backed out of the kitchen door. "Everyone's a comedian."

Slowly the evening wound down, and the crowd

began to thin out. Cindy was loading a tray with dirty glasses when she heard Jan hail her.

"There you are. Good news. I solved your moving problem."

"I told you I'm not comfortable borrowing your friend's truck."

"I know. And I explained that to him. So he offered to drive it himself. Never hurts to have a burly guy around on moving day."

"You asked some stranger to help me move?"

"Relax. He's a nice guy. Besides, he owes me a favor."

"He owes *you* a favor. Not me."

"Cin, lighten up. Let people help you once in a while. Learn to be gracious."

Cindy felt that old familiar panic start to assail her. That terrible feeling that one day she might have to break down and admit she had needs. The feeling struck fear into the deepest, darkest recesses of her soul.

She felt her backbone start to stiffen and pressed her lips tightly closed in case she blurted out something she'd regret a minute later. She loved Jan. And her friend was just trying to help. Still, old habits die hard.

"I don't like being beholden. You, of all people, should understand that."

"I know what drives your stubborn independence. Trust me, it's not one of your more endearing qualities."

"You can't change me, Jan. Love me as I am or let me be."

"You know I love you, girlfriend, but you don't do anything to make it easy."

Cindy knew her sharp tongue had always been her defense against her fear of dependency, and she had learned to wield it effectively over the years to drive a great many people from her life. Anyone who tried to get too close. Except Marissa and a few others. A scant handful of people who needed her more than she needed them.

"Jan, I can't accept a stranger's help."

"Well, I'll leave you to tell him yourself, because here he comes now."

Cindy looked up. The tray of dirty glasses in her hand started to shake.

Making his way across the room toward her and Jan, looking devastatingly handsome in a black tux, was Parker Davis.

"Not... You don't mean Parker Davis, do you?" She forced the words between dry, unresponsive lips.

"You know Parker?" Jan perked right up. "Even better. Then it's not some virtual stranger."

So why did it feel as if a virtual stranger had taken over Cindy's body? A stranger who turned and fled into the kitchen. She set the tray down near the dishwasher knowing full well this wasn't like her to take the coward's way out. To run in the face of adversity.

With renewed determination she straightened, squared her shoulders and tossed her hair back from her face. Head high, she shouldered open the swinging doors into the reception room.

# Chapter Two

Parker watched the leggy blonde make her way through the dwindling crowd toward him and Jan, looking for all the world as if someone had just forced an extremely unpleasant-tasting medicine down her throat.

He'd been busy this evening helping his mother work the room, and hadn't noticed her until Jan had pointed her out. A fact he was instantly ashamed of. He didn't like to think of himself as the type who didn't notice "the help."

Yet the jolt of reaction when he realized who she was prompted his almost eager response to Jan that he'd be more than happy to help her friend move. Now, as he watched her wary approach, he got the distinct impression that his offer of assistance was about to be none-too-gently rebuffed.

"I understand you two have met already," Jan said brightly. The blonde came to a wooden stop next to them, her expression less than delighted.

"Mr. Davis is a Glass Slipper customer," Cindy

said. "Far more formally attired than last time we met."

"You, too," Parker said. He flashed his trademark grin in an effort to put her at ease but, if anything, he could have sworn her spine stiffened even more. "I must say, I prefer your bike shorts."

"Cindy rides her bike everywhere," Jan said. "That's why moving is such a hassle for her."

And why she has such great legs, Parker thought. He stuck out his right hand. "Pleasure to see you again, Cindy."

She stared at his hand as if it were contaminated and she would do anything to avoid the physical contact. Till good manners must have won out. When her fingers brushed his, icy cold to the touch, he resisted the urge to clasp her hand in both of his in an effort to warm it. Even so, he realized he had hung on a little too long when he felt her trying to wriggle her fingers free.

"I trust the new sandals were a hit with your sister?"

"Right on the money," he said.

"My boss is pleased as well. Your patronage pushed store sales to a new high this month."

For not the first time in his life, the awkward moment was salvaged by the arrival of his mother, bless her faultless instincts.

"Jan," she said, "I just wanted to tell you how marvelous the food was. I'm very proud of your business success."

"Thanks, Mrs. Davis."

"How many years now have I been asking you to call me Robin?"

Jan shrugged. "Old habits. Robin, this is my friend Cindy. I couldn't have managed this evening without her."

His mother scored a far more successful handshake than he did, Parker was quick to note. No surprise to see Cindy visibly relax. His mother had that effect on people. He moved closer and looped an arm around his mom's shoulders.

"My date for the evening," he said, just to make it really clear to Cindy that there was no "other date" skulking around waiting for a ride home.

"Parker's dad had a last-minute emergency at the hospital so Parker agreed to come as my escort," Robin said. "Not that I'm not perfectly capable of going places alone, but it's nice to have a designated driver. I'm afraid one glass of wine goes right to my head."

"Don't believe it," Parker scoffed. "She had that alderman eating out of her hand, acting as if her ideas were all his ideas."

"How's Lisa managing at med school?" Jan asked.

"Complaining long and loud about the dreadful hours and the worse hospital food. She's coming back for the wedding."

"I wondered if she might. I'll look forward to catching up with her again."

Parker shot his mother a look, one which she correctly interpreted, for she took Jan's arm. "I'd dearly love to see the kitchen setup you were working with tonight, dear.''

"Oh, um, well…" Clearly it wasn't a request Jan was accustomed to, but she let herself be herded back into the kitchen, leaving Parker alone with Cindy.

Cindy stared at her friend's retreating back like an anguished puppy being left at the pound. Parker decided to make this quick and put her out of her misery.

"Jan said you're moving tomorrow and need a truck. Mine just happens to be free."

"Actually, Mr. Davis, I'm really embarrassed that Jan would put either of us in such an awkward position."

"Parker," he interrupted her.

"Jan had no business making any arrangements on my behalf. Much as I appreciate your kind offer, I really can't accept."

"Listen," he said briskly. "I didn't know it was you, when Jan first mentioned it. But I'm always happy to lend a hand where I can."

"You didn't recognize me earlier this evening?"

"I'm not in the habit of sizing up Jan's assistants, any more than you stand around staring at the suits. Face it, we're both here tonight to perform a function. And that's exactly what we were doing."

"Exactly. Good night, Mr. Davis."

Parker reached out and caught her arm. She didn't feel nearly as frail as she looked. She also didn't seem the type to hang out in the gym. So what did she do to keep in shape besides cycle? It struck him, as he released her, that he wanted to get to know more about her. Much more.

"You helped me out the other day and restored me to hero status in the eyes of my little sister."

"Hero status?"

"You know, the white knight on the charger. My sister believes her big brother should have no other purpose in his life than to come to her rescue. How about you? Any big brother charging to the rescue?"

He knew she didn't have anyone or she wouldn't be stuck trying to move all by herself. As she gave her elegant toffee-colored hair a shake, Parker's fingers itched to muss the tousled curls.

"No brothers. No sisters. Just me."

Parker pulled out a pen and a business card. "Write down your address. I'll be by tomorrow at nine."

Cindy actually planted her hands on her hips and glared at him. "Have you heard a single word I said?"

"Every last one, darlin'. You have no big brother to help you move. So you're stuck with me."

"I don't care to be stuck with you."

He changed tack. Lowered his voice to its most persuasive. "Cindy, you really came through for me the other day in the store. I was in way over my head."

"I was merely doing my job."

"So maybe helping damsels in distress in my spare time is my job."

Her eyes narrowed in such a way Parker knew he'd said the wrong thing, even before she responded.

"Save the act for someone who appreciates it. I'm hardly some frail, helpless damsel in distress. And right now I have a job that needs doing." That said, Cindy turned on her heel and went back to clearing up dirty dishes and crumpled napkins. Parker decided to let her think she'd had the last word.

PARKER LEFT HIS TRUCK in the alley and pushed open the rickety gate to the rear of the apartment block per Jan's instructions. The entire neighborhood had seen better days, especially this building, which had been built in the fifties in the then-popular halfhearted Spanish Mission rip-off. Today it was just a faded reminder of better times, days when the half-dead palm trees had been healthy and vibrant and the cracked and empty swimming pool would have been a hive of activity.

Back in the fifties carloads of folks would have fled Los Angeles to Madronna Beach for long weekends and illicit trysts. In the late sixties a group of hippies had tried to take it over and turn the sleepy town into a commune. Today it was a thriving community, a mix of business people such as himself, artists, students from the nearby college and wealthy retirees with the time and means to golf, support the arts and shop in the ritzy boutiques like the Glass Slipper. Older neighborhoods like this were slowly being restored. All in all, it was a good place to live.

But hardly the type of town he would expect to attract a vibrant young woman like Cindy who, at this particular moment, was running barefoot across the scrubby backyard of the apartment building, in hot pursuit of what appeared to be a limping, squawking duck. Limp or no, the fowl was doing a grand job of eluding Cindy's wildly flapping arms as she tried to corner the creature.

"Close the gate," Cindy yelled, without looking up.

Gate secure, Parker swooped fast and low toward the duck from the opposite direction, a move that did little more than confuse the poor frantic creature. As Cindy moved close, there was a flap of wings and a rain of feathers. Cindy lunged and the duck side-stepped toward Parker, who made a dive for it. With an outraged squawk the duck eluded both of them. They turned in tandem, each took a different approach, and managed to get him cornered.

"Got it!" Parker yelled.

"Got it!" Cindy yelled.

They both dove, collided and wound up on the ground together in a tangle of arms and legs.

Parker was conscious of Cindy sprawled atop him, soft, unbound breasts flattened against his chest, her hair tickling his nose. He felt her elbow near his ribs. Lower down he was aware of the way one of her knees rested a tad too close to a certain area of his body for his comfort. One wrong move and he was a goner.

Except he already was. Instinctively he closed his arms around her. She smelled divine, a blend of sunshine and the ocean and sun-warmed grass. As the sun beat down, cradling them in its warmth, he felt a sudden surge of arousal and had the unmistakable urge to pull her lips down to meet his. To find out if she tasted as sweet as she smelled.

And he well might have. Except for the way she lodged her elbow in his ribs in a move he wasn't at all sure was accidental.

He let out a grunt.

"Sorry." Cindy didn't even pretend to sound contrite as she rolled from his arms and sat up alongside him. "Where's Homer?"

"Who?"

"Homer. The duck."

"He flew over the fence."

"Are you sure?"

Parker pointed to a sprinkling of feathers. "Absolutely."

Cindy rose gracefully to her feet and brushed the dry blades of grass from those incredible legs, displayed to absolute perfection in thigh-hugging black bike shorts. Her feet, as he'd already noticed, were bare except for tarty red polish gleaming on her toenails. Interesting!

"Guess his wing didn't take as long to mend as I thought it would."

"He's not a pet?"

"Nah. Found him on the beach, hurt and covered in oil. A real mess. I brought him home and cleaned him up, but I wasn't sure for a while whether he'd make it or not."

"He wasn't exactly tame and docile, was he?" Parker asked as he got to his feet.

"Never try to tame something wild, Mr. Davis." She leveled him a killer look from those killer green eyes. "What are you doing here?"

"I came to help you move. My truck's in the alley."

He thought for a minute she was going to rehash that old tired "I don't want your help argument," and the crackle of tension between them sounded a new warning when she didn't. Something told him Cindy wasn't one to easily acquiesce.

He followed her into an apartment in the basement, a suite that wasn't even remotely dark and dingy the way he would have thought. Sunlight spilled through clean, undraped windows and shone on glossy white walls. A whimsical waist-high painted border of flowers ringed the wall and led from one room to the next, an effect akin to finding himself in a field of wildflowers. An open window let a fresh breeze blow through the room, and the sun-washed smell reminded him of Cindy. The way she'd felt in his arms.

He gave an appreciative glance. "Nice place. How come you're moving?"

"The landlord didn't like my roommate."

*Her roommate!* Parker felt himself deflate. Did she live with a guy?

"Homer," she added, and Parker couldn't quite credit the buoyant jubilation he felt.

"But Homer's gone."

"And as of today, so am I."

Parker glanced around, but all he saw was a futon,

a boxed-up stereo, a few plastic garbage bags stuffed full and a dozen cartons of books.

"Where's the rest of your stuff?"

"My bike's outside. Other than that, this is it."

"You're kidding."

Cindy pulled on a bulky backpack and adjusted the padded straps on her shoulders. "I told you I could manage on my own."

"Guaranteed to go faster with two. If memory serves me, those futons are a pain to move."

Cindy proved to be remarkably strong for one bordering on slenderness, and in a relatively short time they had hefted her meager pile of belongings into the bed of the pickup. When he went to lift her bike in Cindy stopped him. "I'll ride and meet you there."

Parker had been half expecting just such a move, and couldn't resist meeting the challenge with one of his own.

"Don't tell me you're afraid to be alone with me?"

"Don't be silly."

He indicated the cab of his truck. "I mean, it is pretty close quarters in there."

"I want the exercise."

"You'll get plenty of exercise at the other end unloading this stuff and unpacking."

"Oh, very well." There was nothing gracious in her words or the way she clambered into the truck cab as he stowed her bike with the rest of her stuff. But at least she was in. Parker started the engine and put it into gear. She didn't huddle against her door, and his fingers almost but not quite brushed her left knee. He was wondering if he could somehow arrange contact, pretend to lose his grip, but a sideways look at her face convinced him not to try.

"Where to?"

"What time is it?"

Parker checked his watch. "Ten-fifteen. Why? You have some place to be?"

She flopped back against the seat. "I can't pick up the keys till noon."

The truck idled noisily and Parker wondered what his next logical step ought to be. Offer to buy her breakfast? Somehow he didn't think that would go over any better than the urge he'd had earlier to kiss her. A walk on the pier? That had possibilities, but somehow he didn't see her relaxing and enjoying his company much. Sudden inspiration struck and he eased his foot off the brake.

"Where are we going?" The look she sent him implied she wouldn't be surprised to find herself victim of a kidnapping.

"I couldn't help but notice your library of books on veterinary medicine."

"So?"

"So, I know someone you should meet."

"I already know both the town's vets."

"Tom's a licensed vet, but he doesn't have what one would term a conventional veterinary practice."

She sat up straight and gave him her full attention. Parker congratulated himself for having piqued her interest. "What do you mean?"

"He's a real interesting guy, on contract with the

Department of Wildlife. Been there so long I think they might have forgotten he's on the payroll. I owe him a visit.''

Cindy remained silent as they left Madronna Beach behind. ''He's based out near the canyon,'' Parker offered, in case she wondered where he was taking her. When she gave no indication she'd heard him or cared, Parker slid a country CD into the player and settled back to enjoy the scenery.

Personally he appreciated the company of a woman who didn't feel the need to chatter the entire time, to impress him with her wit and brilliance the way most of the women he met did. Easy silence was what he enjoyed these days. Maybe because he'd never experienced it when he was with Tammy.

He was pushing thirty and knew his parents were proud of him and his business success, but that worried look in his mother's eyes lately meant she was afraid she might never be a grandmother. Truth was, once he'd established the company and adjusted to his single status, he'd ended up having too good a time as a bachelor. Dates were easy enough to come by. Anytime things got too intense from the girl's side he just said his farewells and moved on. He wasn't ready for ''intense.''

Sometime in the last couple of years, Parker wasn't sure exactly when or why, it had stopped being fun and he had lost interest in dating. Maybe because it seemed most females' biological clocks were thumping a lot louder than his own. Suddenly everyone was in a big rush to settle down. Cocooning, it was called.

He had nothing against the "settling down" thing. But he believed everything happened in its own sweet time and he wasn't about to be rushed into something as important as marriage. Or was he simply once bitten, twice shy? Whatever. Already he'd seen several good friends suffer through the pain and upheaval of divorce. Parker knew exactly what he wanted. The same solid, lifelong bond as his parents had. And it wasn't the type of thing he saw as being summoned up at will. Once he thought he'd come close. Had he ever been wrong!

The canyon road was gravel and Parker was glad he'd taken the time to tie down and tarp over Cindy's stuff. The CD ended and he ejected it, no longer needing to fill the silence with more music.

"How'd you wind up in Madronna Beach?" He wasn't merely making conversation. Genuine curiosity prompted the question.

"I grew up here."

"Really?"

"You sound surprised."

"Thought I knew all the locals, that's all."

"My mom was a flower child, born a few years too late to be fashionable."

"Don't tell me there are still folks living out at that old commune to the north."

"Far as I know my mom and her boyfriend and a few others are still there."

"Is that where you grew up?"

"Yup. Mom tried to home-school me, but since she never finished high school herself it wasn't long before I was planning the lessons and doing most of the teaching.''

Cindy paused, and he wondered if that was as much information as she was going to ante up. ''How old were you when you left?''

''Eventually I got so bored out there I moved to town, when I was around fifteen. I was tall enough to lie about my age and get myself a job and an apartment. I spent my spare time up at the college sitting in on whatever classes were going on. Eventually I went for my high school equivalency and last year I got accepted into the college veterinary program.''

''Congratulations!'' His words sounded hollow, at least to him. What Cindy had accomplished was nothing short of miraculous, really. He snuck a quick sideways glance, unable to imagine a life without his mother, father and sister, along with all the security his family's community standing afforded him.

''When do you start your veterinary studies?''

He'd asked the wrong thing; he could tell as soon as the words were out of his mouth. The fact that she'd been knocking around on her own for years explained a lot about her. And the more he learned, the more intrigued he became.

Surely it was more than their differences that intrigued him? The fact that Cindy was so different from the women he usually dated held its own appeal. No denying that. But he'd been drawn to her before he knew a single thing about her. And he wondered how it was their paths had never crossed before.

A few more quiet moments passed before they arrived at Tom's station, or outpost, as he called it. The truck had barely slowed before Cindy opened her door and hopped out. He followed her in a more leisurely fashion to the compound, where an assortment of wounded creatures were caged and convalescing. Cindy reminded him of a kid in a candy store, not knowing where to look first.

"Never know what creatures old Tom will have in his care," Parker said, peering into a cage that housed a baby raccoon.

He glanced at Cindy, gratified to see her face lit up and animated. He'd found her beautiful before. Now she was positively enchanting. He mentally congratulated himself for having the smarts to bring her out here. Right before his eyes she'd turned into a different person, all soft and nurturing, excited as a small kid now that she'd pulled in those thorny barbs she used to protect herself.

"I had no idea this place even existed."

"Most folks haven't got a clue about Tom and the work he does. He does his best to keep it that way."

"Is he around?" She sounded wistful. "Do you think I might get to meet him?"

"Wouldn't surprise me a bit. He'll have seen the truck roll in."

"Parker, you old fool. What brings you out this way?"

Tom Wilson was older than Parker, late thirties by Parker's guesstimate, but he looked years older. His face was deeply creased from years of the sun baking down on him as he tramped the canyons rescuing wounded creatures, cataloging the movements of the local wildlife and the effects of the ever-increasing human population.

"Got somebody here I thought would be interested to meet you and check out your setup. Cindy's got her sights set on vet school."

"Cindy, is it? Tom Wilson." Tom extended his hand toward her in an automatic if seldom-used gesture. Not much call for social niceties living alone out here. Truth be told, he was kind of surprised at Parker, bringing her along. Parker knew he didn't really cotton too much to company. Although the woman before him didn't appear she'd get squeamish at a few animal leavings.

Parker was beaming at her like a kid who'd just opened his favorite toy, and Tom couldn't recall seeing his friend look quite so smitten. Oh, she was a looker all right, but no university cheerleader, if he could still read humans as well as the wild creatures he tended.

"I hope you don't mind us dropping in unannounced," Cindy said with a glance at Parker. "Parker felt sure it would be all right."

"Parker knows I don't serve cookies and lemonade," Tom replied.

"You also don't get enough company to turn anyone away," Parker interjected.

"If nosey-mongers dropped by all the time oohing and aahing, a fellow'd never get a day's work done. Speaking of that, why aren't you at work today?"

"It's Saturday," Parker said quickly. "And I'm helping Cindy move."

"Saturday, is it?" Tom said. He'd never known Parker to take a Saturday off without good reason. So this gal must be the good reason. He turned to Cindy. "Vet school, huh? Isn't no picnic, I can tell you that."

Cindy appeared to stiffen her spine as she spoke. He liked that. "I'm not afraid of hard work."

"Come on, then," Tom said. "You can lend a hand. Both of you."

As he watched the other two set to yakking like long-lost buddies, Parker got the smug feeling that Cindy might have almost forgiven him for blundering in on her this morning and insisting on giving her a hand.

## Chapter Three

"I really liked your friend Tom." Cindy lolled comfortably against the truck's seat back, one bare foot swinging in time to the sultry voice of Michelle Wright. Tom had spoken to her like he would a contemporary, and she was so accustomed to being treated like a clerk or a server it felt really good for a change.

"Couldn't help but notice the way the two of you got along like a house on fire," Parker said.

Cindy straightened. "Do you mind?"

"Mind?" Parker shook his head. "Nothing like the sight of other folks vibrating to something that sparks their cylinders."

"But did you mind that we kind of left you out of a lot of the conversation?"

"Only when you weren't speaking English." Parker flashed her a teasing grin. At least she assumed it was teasing. The guy oozed a lethal amount of charm. Back at her place when they'd collided and rolled on the ground together she'd felt something dangerous, the first faint stirrings of sexual attraction. A minefield she had every intention of steering clear of.

"Have you and Tom been friends for a long time?"

"Has to be ten years or so," Parker said. "He needed some fill trucked in, some other junk hauled away. It was back when he was just getting the place going. I liked him right away and he kind of suffered me." He softened his words with a grin.

"Some people, you just know they're going to stick around in your life awhile. That meeting them has to be more than a chance encounter."

"True enough," Parker agreed. "Somewhat of a risk, though, letting someone that close. Close enough to know who you are way down deep inside."

Cindy didn't bother to respond that she had no intention of letting anyone get that close. "You have to be selective," she said. "You and I, for instance. It's unlikely we'll see each other after today."

"Ships that pass in the night?" Parker said. "Is that your take?"

"Exactly," Cindy said, changing the subject abruptly. "I'm starved. Any chance of my buying you a tube steak on the pier?"

"You bet," Parker said agreeably. Almost too agreeably. Cindy slanted him a searching look. She'd expected him to at least quibble about who paid. She didn't like it when people reacted differently from how she expected. Her radar sent out a loud warning shriek.

Parker took one hand off the wheel and leaned across her, closer than she personally thought necessary, to open the glove compartment. He pulled out a couple of granola bars and dropped one in her lap. "Will this help to tide you over?"

"Thanks." Cindy ripped into the snack and they munched in companionable silence for a few minutes before Parker took a swig of water from a canteen and extended it her way.

As she placed the canteen to her lips and took a grateful sip she realized that her mouth now rested in the same spot his had been only seconds earlier. In spite of herself she recalled those lips near hers as she lay atop him, and the warm rush of his breath across her cheek. The pleasant way it had felt to have his arms close around her. Not at all restrictive like she would have expected, but actually comfortable, supportive. A little too nice. Which is why she'd pretended to accidentally dig him in the ribs with her elbow. It wouldn't do to start feeling too comfortable with any man's arms around her.

"So tell me about Parker Davis." Her voice sounded brittle in her ears, almost shrill, and she tried to temper it. "I take it you grew up in Madronna Beach, as well."

"Yup."

"Let me guess." Cindy rested her head back and half closed her eyes in concentration. "Your dad's something important. A lawyer?"

"G.P.," Parker said.

"I knew it. You grew up in one of those big fancy houses in the hills with a swimming pool and a killer view and a gardener. Your mom devoted herself to you kids and dabbled in the arts.''

"Mom did her own gardening. She's head of the local horticulture society. In fact, she's the one who got it started."

"Still..." Cindy couldn't keep the note of triumph from her voice. "You had the traditional upper-class family upbringing with all the privileges that background brings. I bet you were a football hero. And valedictorian of your graduating class."

"What are you? Psychic?"

"Why didn't you go into medicine?"

"Didn't hold my interest. My sister's the one in med school."

"So you're the family black sheep. Make that blue-collar sheep."

Parker wheeled into a parking spot at the pier. "Nothing ever turned me on the way trucks do. Apparently *truck* was the first word that came out of my mouth, much to my mom's disappointment." He laughed, a rich masculine rumble that sounded as if it came from somewhere intimately low in his body. "I was lucky I had parents who encouraged me to be my own person."

Cindy bent down and slid her bare feet into her flat, sensible sandals. By the time she was done Parker had come around and opened the truck door for her, and she wasn't sure if she liked his old-fashioned courtesy or not. The truck was high, and as she slid from the seat, the heel of her sandal got caught. She stumbled and managed, despite her best efforts not to, to fall against him.

"You okay?" He caught and held her while she found her balance.

"A curse of having such big feet," Cindy said. "They make me clumsy." She straightened. The touch of his strong, capable fingers on her arms lingered in an unsettling manner.

She tried to pull free. Parker detained her. Subjected her to a too-close scrutiny. "You're not clumsy. And I'd have to say you're about perfectly balanced on those gorgeous feet of yours."

Cindy wriggled out of his arms and decided then and there to order extra onions on her tube steak. She wondered if Mr. Rich-kid Davis had ever eaten anything as lowly as a jumbo hot dog while hanging over the pier railing.

Her musings were put to rest when an apron-clad Jules, the hot dog maestro of Madronna Beach, greeted Parker by name. Not only did Jules know Parker, it was pretty darn obvious he liked him. Everyone, it seemed, liked Parker Davis.

So why did the back of her neck bristle every time he stepped close? Or was it a tingle? It was a bristle, she decided. An internal warning she would do well to pay heed to.

"Any news on the shoe front?" Jules asked as he swapped her tube steak for cash. She shook her head and shot a glance to Parker, who was smearing his tube steak with spicy Dijon.

"Keeping my eyes and ears open for you," Jules said.

"Thanks, Jules." She cast him a grateful smile, rewarded by an earsplitting grin from the hunched and grizzled ex-New Yorker. He'd come to her rescue once, years earlier, and the two of them had formed a friendship of sorts, even though neither of them ever spoke about that night.

"How's the trucking biz, Parker?"

"Probably not near as lucrative as this money-maker you've got here," Parker said, in what Cindy interpreted to be a long-standing banter between the two men.

"Anytime you want to trade hats," Jules said.

"Hey, anyone can drive a truck," Parker said. "Nobody else can make these taste the way you do."

"Enjoy," Jules said, turning to greet his next customer.

They moved out of the line of foot traffic, farther down the pier. Parker leaned against the railing next to her, his hip all but locked against hers. Impossible to eat without their arms brushing. She decided to ignore him, if such a thing was possible.

"Jules makes the best dogs in the west," Parker said, taking a bite. She could feel the warmth from his body seep toward her, in contrast to the brisk ocean breeze that ruffled her unruly hair. The sun tended to bleach the top layers a pale wheat and leave the underneath hair dark gold. Once she had contemplated touching it up, to try to achieve an even tone, but in the end decided not to tamper with nature.

"You cold?"

He laid a fist across her forearm and lightly smoothed the goose bumps that peppered her tanned skin.

"No. I love the wind. It's so, I don't know. Natural. Unstoppable. Free."

"Aren't you free?"

"Not yet." But someday, Cindy vowed. Free from the stigma of her untraditional upbringing. Free from her fears of needing anyone.

The ocean lapped at the pier's pilings with gusto. A short distance from shore the breakers were peppered with the brightly colored wet suits of the surfers.

Parker balled his napkin and tossed it in the trash. "You ready?"

"Of course." Cindy popped the last bite of hot dog into her mouth and followed him back to the truck. "I didn't intend to take up your whole day. I mean, you probably have other things you'd rather be doing."

"Actually, you didn't take up any of my day that I didn't want you to." He opened the truck door and in a totally unexpected move planted his hands around her waist, picked her up and lifted her inside.

Cindy let out an outraged squawk, which he misinterpreted as gratitude.

"'Welcome," he said, then loped around the front of the truck and climbed behind the wheel. He turned to face her, his right arm resting disturbingly close to her along the seat back. "Thanks for the lunch. Now, where to?"

Cindy mumbled directions to her new apartment, feeling at a decided disadvantage. Anything she might say, such as taking him to task for the way he'd lifted her into the truck, was bound to make her sound petty and churlish. She decided once more to ignore him. But Parker Davis was not an easy man to ignore.

She picked up the keys from the super and, Parker at her heels toting a carton of books, unlocked the door to an apartment that was nearly identical to the one she had just vacated.

Except that she'd have to start all over again. The walls were a dingy mustard yellow. Sagging gold curtains kept the sunlight at bay.

"You sure have got the library," Parker said as he piled a final carton of books in the front room.

"They're a pain to move," Cindy said.

"Worth it if they're important to you."

His words caused a ripple of gratitude to wash through her. No one else ever seemed to understand just how important her books were. She didn't care if she had new clothes. She existed quite happily without a TV and VCR. But take away her books and she would literally shrivel up and die.

Parker peered into an open-ended box. "Some of them look quite old."

"I buy secondhand usually. Estate sales and stuff. Library discards." Her thrifty habits probably sounded stupid to him. If he wanted a book he only had to stroll into any of a dozen specialized bookstores in town and order whatever he wanted.

"I love old books. Look at the inscription in this one." He'd picked up a worn copy of *Indiana* by George Sand, opened the cover and let out a low whistle. "Copyright, 1832. To Tessa. Love always, Thaddeus. On our anniversary. May 1927."

He closed the book and ran his thumb reverently down the spine. "Little piece of history, right here in your hand."

Parker glanced around and frowned. "You really ought to have bookshelves, you know."

Cindy shrugged. "Given a choice of buying books or shelves to stick them on, I go for the books every time."

Parker grinned. "I'm surprised you don't work in a bookstore."

"I wouldn't dare! Do you know how broke I'd be? Every payday I'd owe them money. I'd never get to vet school."

His grin widened. "Most women would feel that about the shoe palace where you work."

"Shoes. After a while you get sick of them. I mean, they're only something to walk in, right?"

"Yoo-hoo! Cindy! Are you in there?"

Cindy pushed past Parker and bolted up the few concrete steps to the walkway. "Rissa. Did you wheel yourself all this way?"

Marissa bent one arm at the elbow—Popeye-style, flexing her biceps. "Just because I'm paraplegic doesn't mean I can sit around getting fat. I exercise the same as everyone else. Besides," she said waving a letter in her other hand. "Good news! Someone found the Louboutin."

"Really?" Cindy squealed. "For sure?"

"He sent a picture and everything." Her face crumpled. "There's one catch."

"What's that?"

"He doesn't want the reward. He wants a date with Cinderella."

"Seriously?"

"That's what he says."

"You'll have to play the part of Cinderella," Cindy said flatly. "I'll take you. He can place the shoe on your foot, or whatever fantasy fetish he's angling for."

Marissa's face fell. "We both know I'm not Cinderella. You are."

"Bibbidy-bobbedy-boo," Cindy said crossly.

"It's probably rude of me to ask, but what's a Louboutin?"

Cindy whirled. She'd forgotten all about Parker. He leaned against the stairwell wall, an amused smile on his face. Marissa caught sight of him and turned bright red.

"You should have told me you had company."

"Parker Davis is helping me move. Parker, meet my friend Marissa."

"Aka Cinderella?" Parker asked, coming forward to shake Marissa's hand.

"That's Cindy's moniker, not mine."

His grin widened and Cindy would have happily

wiped it from his face. "You mean Cindy's short for Cinderella?" He gave her an infuriating smile. "I had no idea."

Cindy stuck out a bare foot. "Some joke. With skis this size."

Marissa gave Parker a patient look. "Cindy thinks she has big feet."

"I was just telling her they look perfectly in proportion to the rest of her. You coming in to check out the new digs?"

Marissa seemed to shrink a little in her chair. "I can't. The stairs."

"Nothing a strong pair of arms can't solve. May I?" Parker effortlessly lifted Marissa in his arms. "Cindy can bring your chair down."

Cindy saw the hesitation flit across her friend's face. "Do you mind, Cin?"

"Not at all. I was hoping to find a ground-level entry so we can visit back and forth more easily. But I'm running out of apartments in town."

"Cindy gets evicted on a regular basis," Marissa told Parker.

"Really? Is she a bad tenant?"

"No, she's wonderful. But she has this habit of collecting strays, contrary to the no-pets rules."

"Ah, like Homer," Parker observed.

"Yes. Where is Homer?"

"He, ah, flew the coop today, so to speak."

"He's all better? That's wonderful."

Cindy couldn't believe her ears at Marissa's easy

chatter with Parker. Usually her friend was quite reticent around new people. Until she got to know them, at least. After that, look out! But with Parker there'd been none of that wariness or silence she was used to witnessing—Marissa's way of getting a sense of a new person before she opened up to them. Instead, she was acting as if she and Parker had been best friends for years.

With a minimum of fuss Parker carried Marissa inside and settled her back in her chair. "Nice shoes," he said, bending down to admire the leopard-print mules.

Marissa beamed. "Isn't it fun? I love shoes. And thanks to Cindy I—"

Cindy interrupted before Marissa could divulge their secret. "I hope you're going to help me paint again. Those wildflowers were like magic in the old place."

"Of course."

"Great," Cindy said. She marched across the room and tugged open the ugly yellow curtains, resisting the urge to rip them from their rods. Unfortunately the sunshine made everything in the room appear even shabbier, if such a thing was possible.

Parker straightened up. "So back to my original question. What's a Louboutin? And who has it? Sounds like something from the Maltese Falcon."

Before Cindy could stop her, Marissa passed the snapshot to Parker. "That's the Louboutin. Three hundred dollars for the pair, aren't they, Cin?"

Parker whistled. "At that price he could just about hold it for ransom."

"The left one went missing and we have to get it back before Cindy's boss notices it's gone."

"Marissa!" Cindy injected a warning note into her tone.

"Someone stole one shoe?"

"Cindy dropped it. On her way to my place."

Parker's gaze found Cindy's. In spite of herself she felt the heat of a flush creep up her neck to her cheeks, fueled by the look in those knowing blue eyes. To her immense relief he didn't pursue the topic. He turned to Marissa. "You going to stay here and help Cindy unpack?"

She nodded. "I'd like that."

"I'll stop back in about an hour and see how things are going."

"You don't have to do that," Cindy said quickly.

"Cindy," Marissa said firmly. "Yes, he does. Unless you want me here permanently."

"Right," Cindy said with what she acknowledged was poor grace. Parker didn't seem to notice. He appeared intent on getting out of there as quickly as he could.

PARKER RETURNED to Cindy's apartment and started to unload his truck, knowing full well he was about to have an altercation on his hands. The woman was pricklier than a porcupine, proud as an eagle and stubborn as a mule. He caught himself and grinned. Must be all that vet talk earlier between her and Tom that had him with animals on the brain.

He found the girls in the living room unpacking books, and was happy to see those dingy gold drapes had disappeared. Already the place seemed bigger and brighter. Quietly he snuck the groceries he'd bought into Cindy's empty fridge.

Then he went outside and plugged in his skilsaw.

He had barely made two cuts when Cindy came flying out the door the way he knew she would, her mouth moving a mile a minute. He couldn't hear her over the noise of the saw and his earmuffs, but he could read the righteous indignation on her face clearly enough. Her lips moved again, their message plain.

"What are you doing?"

He turned off the saw and removed his earmuffs and safety goggles. He stared hard at her. She damn well could see exactly what he was doing. He said nothing, just waited, watching her internal struggle. Habit won out. She wasn't accustomed to accepting help. Not from any quarter. Something he'd already figured out and decided to ignore.

"I know what you're up to. And I appreciate the gesture, really I do. But I refuse—"

"You don't have the right to refuse."

"This is my apartment. My home."

"I'm doing this for your friend. She needs you."

"Rissa and I will figure out something. On our own. The way we always have."

"So it's all right for you to sneak a three-hundred-dollar pair of shoes out of the shop to put a smile on your friend's face. But it's not all right for me to spend a couple of hours building a ramp so she can get in and out of your apartment under her own steam and feel more independent. Where's the logic?"

"Logic?" Cindy sputtered.

"You of all people ought to understand how important Marissa's independence is to her. And your friendship."

"I do. I just don't happen to like being beholden to a stranger."

"We can fix that."

"How?" Her eyes darkened with suspicion. Parker wondered how long it would take him to wipe away that distrust. To see her eyes glow with happiness and laughter. To hear her break down and laugh out loud.

"Have dinner with me tonight."

"I have plans," Cindy said.

"Change them."

"I can't."

"Can't or won't?"

"Take your pick."

"Then you leave me no choice."

"No choice?"

"No choice but to do something so you quit calling me a stranger."

Parker took his time as he pulled Cindy into his arms. He wanted to enjoy the feeling of her pressed up tight against him. Anticipate the taste of her lips beneath his. Not until he had her settled, noticed just how right she felt in his arms, did he tip her head back and cover her warm, full lips with his own.

## Chapter Four

To Cindy's deep dismay, there was something nice about finding herself trussed up against Parker, being stroked and caressed by his wonderful, capable hands. Finally he let her go. She stepped back a pace, unable to still the relief that rushed through her. If he'd held her much longer she'd have been tempted to remain there, snug in his embrace.

"Was that supposed to prove something?" Her riotous feelings made her voice sharper than necessary.

Parker just slanted her a bemused look. "You can't keep calling me a stranger now that we've kissed."

"We haven't kissed," Cindy said. "You kissed me. I didn't kiss you back. There's a world of difference."

"Don't I know it."

Much as she hated to back down from a standoff, Cindy turned and walked back into the apartment. Behind her she heard the saw start up again. Usually a withering glance and a well-chosen caustic remark ensured that any man who got in her face when she didn't want him there turned tail and fled. So why not

Parker? Balls of steel, she decided. Coupled with an ego the size of the blue Pacific. He was going to be darn hard to get rid of. Hard but not impossible.

She smiled to herself. Over the years, since that night on the beach when Jules had rushed to her aid, she had become a bona fide pro at fending off unwanted advances. Since the Miss Chill routine didn't appear to have any discernible impact on Parker Davis, she'd simply try a different tack. Act all clingy and dependent and helpless, a move that ought to send him hightailing for cover.

"What a nice guy Parker is," Marissa said, for what had to be the fortieth time that afternoon.

"Prince Charming in the flesh," Cindy muttered, talking around the nail in her mouth as she struggled to hang her one original framed painting.

"Up a little," Marissa said, head cocked. "Too much. Now over. Wrong way. The left corner is too low. Raise it up a bit."

"Oh, for pity's sake." Cindy lowered the heavy painting to the floor and rubbed her aching shoulders.

"Allow me?" Once again, Parker was there to rescue her. He took the hammer out of her hand and claimed the nail from between her lips. He positioned the painting.

"How's that?"

"Perfect," Marissa said, clapping her hands.

He made everything look so damn easy, right down to hanging a picture. Cindy had no use for a man who thought his maleness commanded him the God-given right to see and conquer.

*Sweet,* she reminded herself. Be so sweet you'll make his teeth ache. "Saccharine" him right out of here for good.

"Oh, Parker, thank you so much. I don't know how I would have managed if you hadn't come along just then and taken care of things for me." She almost winced at the simpering tone in her voice. Even Marissa sent her a funny look. Tone it down! she commanded herself. The man isn't stupid.

Parker just gave her a companionable wink. "Sure you do. Same way as always." He turned to Marissa. "Want to take the ramp for a test-drive?"

Marissa scooted up and down the new ramp a few times and pronounced it just right, waving her goodbyes behind her.

Now was her big chance. Squashing down any hesitancy, Cindy turned to Parker. "Still want to have that dinner tonight?"

Parker appeared deeply engrossed in packing away his tools and sweeping up bits of sawdust from the stairs.

"'Fraid I'll have to take a rain check. Some other time?"

"Sure," Cindy said, feeling somewhat deflated and not nearly as relieved as she would have thought. "Some other time."

It was hours later before hunger drove her in the direction of the fridge. As she opened the door and came face-to-face with further evidence of Parker's thoughtfulness she felt a small wave of shame sweep through her. She owed the man more than thanks; she owed him an apology. And she *always* paid her debts.

MARISSA STARED OUT the window of the county van transporting her to the Hunter Green Ranch. As always, she was grateful not to remember the motor vehicle accident that had killed both her parents and left her in a wheelchair. She'd been four at the time and mercifully recalled nothing.

She'd been raised by a spinster aunt and bachelor uncle who had no clue about children or their need for love. Fortunately there'd been money from the insurance settlement, and physically, at least, she'd wanted for nothing. Her life had been busy with horseback riding lessons, pool therapy, fancy summer camps and expensive boarding schools.

It had been a shock at age seventeen to learn the money was gone due to poor investments and lavish living. She'd used the last few remaining dollars for art school tuition and the down payment on her tiny house here in Madronna Beach.

But she'd missed riding, and one day, with more nerve than a toothache, she'd arranged a ride to the ranch, where she had offered to teach children to ride in exchange for saddle time for herself.

She'd never know if it was pity or need that caused Ruth, perennially fifty-something with leathery skin, a gravelly voice and cropped gray hair, to accept her offer. But it had worked out. Marissa thoroughly enjoyed being outside, back in the saddle, and working with the kids.

A new group was starting today and Marissa always thanked heaven for her gift of patience. As usual the kids just wanted to jump on and ride, not learn a proper seat, hold and heels.

"Cameron," she called out. "Heels down. Head up. That's it. Feel yourself become one with Bailey."

Ruth had taken her aside earlier and told her Cameron had been diagnosed with attention deficit disorder and his parents held the hope that, given his love for horses, riding lessons might assist him to focus. Cameron was a challenging student, but Marissa knew how difficult the world could be for anyone who seemed even a little bit different.

"Very good!" She rode up next to him and gave him an encouraging thumbs-up. "Now watch me."

She rode into position, took her time to make sure she was as ready as her mount, then urged Cappuccino forward in the direction of the hunter-jumper bar. Just as they started to jump she glimpsed the butterfly from the corner of one eye, a flutter of yellow-and-black wings. It's presence was just enough to spook Cappuccino, who at the last second failed to clear the bar. Marissa was spooked herself, just enough to lose her seat and land in a cloud of dry dirt with the wind knocked from her lungs.

As she fought to breathe, telling herself not to panic, she was aware of a strange man kneeling at her side. He had the kindest gray eyes she had ever looked into, eyes that had clearly seen more than their share of sadness but hadn't hardened their owner.

He placed a hand on her shoulder and his touch warmed her. "Are you all right?"

She nodded, unable to speak.

"Lucky it wasn't a bad spill."

He rose and approached Cappuccino, who stood a short distance away, watching warily. A few words to Cameron and Bailey, a soft croon to Cappuccino, and all was calm within the riding ring. The stranger captured Cappuccino's reins and brought her to Marissa's side.

"I wager she's more upset that you were unseated than you are," he said, standing alongside her. When she didn't move he reached down a hand to her.

"I'm afraid I can't get up on my own," Marissa said with quiet dignity.

He hunkered down alongside her, concern softening the texture of his skin. She was still having trouble catching her breath, but for an entirely different reason. "Are you hurt?"

She shook her head.

"How can I help?"

Marissa warmed to the way he looked at her. She felt captured in his gaze, caught up in something she never wanted to escape from.

He cleared his throat. "Please forgive me for staring, but I've never seen anyone with quite your luminous beauty."

Marissa smiled. "Usually people stare at me for a whole different reason."

"And what reason might that be?"

"I'm paraplegic." She stated it as matter-of-factly as if announcing she was left-handed.

The man before her didn't drop her gaze. His eyes didn't cloud over with sympathy or discomfort the way most people's did.

"My name's Tom." He extended his right hand toward her. "What's your name, beautiful lady?"

"Marissa." Her hand slid into his as if it belonged there. She couldn't tear her gaze from his.

"Like I said before, what can I do to help?"

The moment was interrupted by the arrival of Ruth and her husband, who clucked and fussed and, after being reassured that she was perfectly all right, got her situated back in the saddle.

By the time she looked around Tom was gone, and she couldn't explain the ping of disappointment racing through her.

"Ruth, who was that nice man?"

"You mean Tom? He's an old buddy of Gil's. A licensed vet. He no longer has a practice, but Gil still calls him in anytime there's a complication with one of the horses. Says Tom has a right calming way about him."

"He certainly has that," Marissa agreed. Then she turned her attention back to her pupil. "That, Cameron, was most definitely not the way to make your jump."

CINDY LOOKED UP when the shop bell rang and nearly dropped the stack of shoe boxes balanced in her arms.

*Melody Manners,* Miss Scoop-Snoop from the *Madronna Beach Review.*

Shopping for new footwear? Not likely! The woman lived in army boots and fatigues. Clearly she envisioned herself as a journalist in some war-torn Third World nation, rather than scratching around trying to invent news where there was none in sleepy little Madronna Beach.

"Cindy!" Melody's enthusiasm sounded as forced as the reporter looked. "I was hoping we could have a word."

"Kinda busy," Cindy mumbled as she headed for the storeroom. Melody, of course, followed.

"I've made a few inquiries," Melody said. "Readers are really intrigued by the Cinderella Saga."

"The what?" Cindy decided to play dumb.

"The hunt for the missing shoe and its return to its rightful owner. Everyone's following the notes in the paper."

Cindy methodically returned the shoe boxes to their correct shelf location. If even one pair got out of place it presented a bona fide disaster for their upcoming inventory.

"Can't you go chase an ambulance, Mel, like a good reporter?"

"Do you deny being the Cinderella of the ads?"

"Vehemently." Cindy pushed past the other woman to the front of the shop.

"Well, I'm doing a story, anyway. I sure could use a few good quotes to give it some zing."

"Such as?"

Melody whipped out her notebook. "How about 'Fairytales do come true, our Cinderella says with a serene smile, as her prince slips the lost shoe onto the foot of its rightful owner'?"

Cindy swung around and faced the reporter. "Mel, do your research. The missing shoe is what size?"

"Eight, narrow," Mel said huffily. "I do my research."

Cindy kicked off her sandal, picked it up and held it out for Melody's inspection. "Size ten, medium. I haven't worn a size eight since I was nine years old."

Melody seemed to visibly deflate, then she brightened. "But you must know who Cinderella is. You would have sold her the shoes in the first place."

Cindy waved a hand to encompass the entire Glass Slipper's floor-to-ceiling inventory. "Do you have any idea how many customers come through this door in a day? Do you really think I have the time or the energy to remember them all? To remember any of them?"

"Can I quote you?" Melody asked.

"What? 'Shoe clerk unable to recall identity of mystery shopper.' Absolutely not! There is no story here and I refuse to help you invent one."

"What about a quote as an anonymous source?"

"What about you go hustle up some real news?"

"This is news," Melody said. "This could be the big break I need."

Cindy gently but firmly herded Melody toward the door. "If I think of anything helpful, I'll call you. Honest." Just then a tour bus disgorged its passengers right out front. In seconds the shop was overrun and Melody and her story were pushed clear out of Cindy's head.

NORMALLY CINDY WASN'T the nervous type. And the pier at sunset was hardly a menacing rendezvous point. Still, she couldn't repress a shiver as she sat barefoot on the far bench awaiting the arrival of Mr. Louboutin. Their back-and-forth correspondence via the newspaper personal column, coupled with desperation to retrieve the pump, had resulted in her sitting here barefoot as per instructions, praying that by the end of the evening the red pump was back in her possession.

The finder had dismissed any talk of a reward other than this meeting, which led Cindy to wonder just how he might expect to be recompensed for the shoe's safe return.

There was no need to feel even the slightest twinge of nerves. Madronna Beach was a small town. Chances were good she knew whoever had found the shoe. They'd share a laugh over the situation and go their separate ways. Besides, if she'd given in to Marissa's offer to come with her, her dear friend would have only been a liability in this instance. Parker, now, she wouldn't mind Parker's reassuring presence....

Cindy gave herself a mental shake. She had to stop thinking about Parker Davis. He was creeping into her thoughts way too often lately. Ever since he'd kissed her. What had he been trying to prove? Other than his irresistibility to the opposite sex.

The town clock struck nine, startling Cindy from her thoughts about Parker. Moments later a figure slunk out of the shadows and started toward her. Cindy knotted and unknotted her fingers, relieved to note the fellow was slight rather than burly and quite hunched-shouldered. As he drew close she heaved a sigh. It was Mr. Hubble, the town eccentric, who lived in a huge run-down house with about a million cats. Elusive but harmless, he rarely came out of his house during the day but could often be seen scuttling around in the early dusk. Figured. It had been dusky out the day she lost the shoe.

He approached hesitantly and stopped. He licked his lips. "Cinderella?"

"It's me, Mr Hubble. Cindy from the shoe store."

"Cinderella," he said, sinking to his knees before her and attempting to slide the pump onto her bare foot. Predictably, it was several sizes too small and wouldn't fit.

"Ow!" Cindy said when he gave her foot a twist, trying to jam it into the pump.

He reared back. "You're not Cinderella! You're an imposter! This shoe only fits my Cinderella."

All of a sudden pandemonium erupted on the pier. A flash bulb exploded. Mr. Hubble roared his displeasure and took off with the shoe. Cindy leapt to her feet, prepared to give chase, only to be detained by Melody from the local paper.

"Melody," she wailed. "You scared him off. I never got the shoe."

Melody shrugged. "Sorry, Cin. But like I told you earlier, it's great human interest. Everyone in town's been following the story in the ads. They all want to know about Cinderella meeting her prince. And I knew you just had to be involved somehow."

Cindy grabbed Melody's arm. "Mr. Hubble is hardly anyone's Prince Charming. He's just a harmless, lonely eccentric."

"Clearly one who believes in destiny and happy endings. Otherwise he never would have shown up. The readers will gobble this up."

Cindy crossed her arms over her chest. "I mean it, Melody. Run that picture and I'll sue the pants off of you and the paper."

"You wouldn't have the means."

"But I do."

Cindy's heart sank, hearing Parker's voice from the shadows behind her.

"Listen to Cindy's point of view, Melody. Not even you want to be responsible for someone losing their job. Which is exactly what'll happen if you insist on publicizing this. It's a small town, Mel. Doesn't take much to ruin someone. Even a reporter."

Melody glanced behind Cindy and her entire expression lit up. Clearly the woman was too enthralled by Parker's presence to even hear the underlying threat in his words.

"Parker. I haven't seen you in way too long."

He held out his hand. "Give me the film, Melody. Away from temptation and all that."

Melody's grip on her camera tightened perceptibly. Abruptly she relented, a provocative look crossing her face as she surrendered the camera. "You know, I never could refuse you a thing, you rat."

Her words were fraught with double entendre, which Parker didn't bother to respond to. He simply opened the camera, pulled out the film and handed it back to her.

"You did the right thing. You'll be able to sleep tonight."

Melody sashayed forward till she was practically joined at the hip with him. "I know one sure-fire guarantee of how I'd sleep a whole lot better."

When Parker didn't bite, Melody shrugged and made her exit, leaving Cindy to feel as if she'd been invisible during the entire exchange. Watching Melody's retreating back, Cindy turned to Parker. "Is there a woman in this town you haven't slept with?"

"One or two," Parker said easily. "You had no business coming down here by yourself after dark."

"I'm surprised the whole town wasn't here with a brass band," Cindy muttered. "Who told you where I'd be? Marissa?"

"She was right to be worried. You leave Hubble to me. I'll get the shoe back for you first thing tomorrow."

Cindy felt a surge of annoyance. "You will do no

such thing. I'll get it back myself, now that I know where it is and who has it.''

"Cindy, I've had dealings with Hubble before. He's unpredictable. As likely to flush the thing down the toilet as pass it over to you.''

"And that would be my problem, then. Wouldn't it?''

Parker bit back an exasperated sigh. "Do you ever miss the opportunity to make life harder than it needs to be?''

"And miss out on any of life's challenges? Never.''

"That's exactly what I thought you'd say.'' Ruefully he shook his head. "Will you at least humor me and allow me to see you home safely?''

He really was intent on his white-knight role, Cindy thought. And he wore it well. She was loath to admit it, but she wasn't as dismayed by his presence as she ought to be.

"Can we stop by Hubble's on the way?''

"Haven't you had enough excitement for one day? Besides, he'll have gone into hiding. Catch him off guard tomorrow.''

"I suppose you're right.'' Reluctantly Cindy followed Parker to his truck, aware that she now owed him an even greater debt. "I do owe you a big thank-you for scaring Melody off the story.''

"I wouldn't have minded so much if I'd been the one sliding the famed glass slipper onto Cinderella's dainty bare foot.'' Parker sounded so wistful that Cindy did a double take.

"Don't tell me you believe in fairy tales, too? First Hubble, now you. It's really too much for a girl to take in."

"Hey, my folks were high school sweethearts, still madly in love thirty-five years later. It's quite the act to try to emulate."

"Little late for you to hook up with your high school sweetheart," Cindy said. "Or maybe not. Is little Miss Head Cheerleader still on the scene?"

"She was a gymnast," Parker said. "A very good one."

Omigod. It was written all over his face. The man was still carrying a torch for his high school love. Why did the sudden realization not sit well with her?

"The love of your life, from the sounds of it," Cindy said lightly.

"I thought so at the time," Parker said. "Fate decreed otherwise. She was intent on slowly destroying herself, although at the time she couldn't see it."

"And you couldn't save her," Cindy said under her breath, so softly she knew Parker couldn't hear her. Hence the crusader unleashed, still trying to save those damsels in distress.

She faced him and raised her voice. "Frankly, Parker, I don't know what to think. I ought to be furious with you and your bad habit of butting into my affairs."

The grin he shot her was cocky with off-kilter charm. "Seems to be the only way I can grab your sure-fire attention."

"Why do you want my attention?"

"Bad habit of mine. Wanting what I can't have."

Like happily ever after, and white picket fences and his high school love? Cindy wondered. She knew better than to ever hanker after what she couldn't have. Vet school was a challenge, but a reachable goal. Were these rich boys all the same? Only desiring her because she remained unattainable?

On the way to Cindy's apartment, Parker insisted on stopping for Chinese takeout. Without waiting to be asked he followed her in, where he stopped short just inside the door and let out a low, admiring whistle.

"You should be an interior decorator."

"Not me, Marissa. It's all her doing. She's a whiz with a paintbrush. Not to mention the sewing machine. She covered all these pillows for me." Cindy bent to light a cluster of votive candles on the coffee table, then indicated the oversize floor cushions that she used instead of furniture. "Pull up a seat. You want a Heineken?"

"Sure. My favorite."

"Yeah, well, it seems a six-pack came with the apartment." He followed her into the tiny kitchen, where she pulled two long-necked green bottles from the fridge, removed the caps and handed one to Parker.

As if they'd eaten together dozens of time, he went ahead with the Chinese food while she fetched plates and chopsticks, carried them to the table and pulled a cushion up next to him. "That was a very thoughtful thing that you did. Stocking the fridge the day I moved in.''

Parker clinked the neck of his beer bottle against hers. ''Somebody did the same thing for me once on moving day. I never forgot how good it made me feel.''

Cindy studied his face in the flickering candlelight, impressed that he hadn't shrugged off his gesture with an ''Aw, shucks. It was nothing.''

''I'm not accustomed to people doing things like that for me. I don't really know how to respond.''

He picked up a cardboard container of prawns and spooned some onto her plate. ''You're doing just fine.''

Cindy felt herself color at his words. Why did she feel uncomfortable with the situation at hand? She and Parker, side by side. Candles. Beer. Chinese food. She jumped to her feet.

''Where are you going?''

''Music,'' she said.

Parker caught her wrist and tugged her back down next to him. ''Is that so you don't have to talk to me?''

''No. Yes. Maybe.'' When she realized she was toying with a wisp of hair near her ear she pulled her hand back as if burned. She wasn't about to take on a sudden nervous habit around Parker. No way on earth.

Parker just shook his head slowly. ''What did I do to make you so uncomfortable?''

"Same thing you're doing right now," Cindy said. "You say exactly what's on your mind."

"It's the best way I know to avoid misunderstandings."

Cindy gave a short laugh. "See? And I've always found that avoiding people is my best way to steer clear of misunderstandings."

Try as she might Cindy was unable to back down from the deep sea of knowing in Parker's blue eyes. "You don't avoid people," he said with typical bluntness. "You avoid closeness. You keep everyone at arm's length."

Cindy resisted the urge to shift away from him, out of range of that scrumptious body and those all-knowing eyes. Instead she picked up the bottle and took a healthy swig from her beer. "Can we change the topic?"

"Sure. Congratulations on finding out who has the shoe."

Cindy blew out a long breath. "Thanks. I have to admit I'll rest easier once it's back in stock."

"You really shouldn't have gone down there by yourself."

"Save us both the lecture. I do everything by myself."

"But it isn't always necessary."

"How do you know? What gives you the right to judge what I ought to do and how I ought to do it?"

Parker pushed their plates to one side and leaned toward her. Too close. He cupped her cheek in his hand and gently stroked her cheekbone with the tips of his fingers. She ought to pull away. But his touch was hypnotic. Warm. Comforting. She wanted more. Human warmth and comfort.

She licked her suddenly dry lips. "Don't."

"Don't what?" When he traced the outline of her ear his touch made her nerve endings tingle up and down the column of her neck.

She reached up to push his hand away. Instead, she covered it with her own. Outlined each oversize knuckle on the back of his hand. It had been so long since she'd been touched. So long since a man had looked at her with the admiration and interest that she saw reflected in Parker's eyes. So long since human touch had the power to warm her clear through. To reach that frozen spot inside her that never seemed to get warm.

When Parker stroked her face, her lips parted as if by magic. Gently she took his fingertips, one at a time between her lips, in a half kiss, half nibble. At the same time he outlined the shape of her lips, his fingers stroking her as if she was the most fragile, the most resonant of any delicately strung instrument.

This time it was she who reached out to him. She who clasped the back of his neck and drew his head down. She who opened her mouth, wanting, needing his kiss. Waiting with openmouthed anticipation for the divine pressure of his lips meeting hers. It was more than a kiss. It was a heart-stopping experience. A feast. His mouth shaped itself to hers as naturally as if they'd been doing it this way forever. There was no awkwardness, no bumping of noses, no repositioning. Merely a deep and abiding sense that she was about to experience something new and wonderful. Something she'd waited for her entire life.

Fear and exhilaration coursed through her. She cupped his face, holding him close, and felt the faint abrasion of the day's growth of whiskers beneath her palms. A blatant reminder of his maleness, which spiraled through her to create new waves of want.

Their breathing merged and became one. As the kiss deepened, tension flowed through her. Cindy eased backward and Parker followed till she reclined atop a pile of pillows. He pushed her T-shirt out of the way and found her small, perfectly shaped breasts, nipples tight and aching for his touch. She jerked when the tip of his tongue grazed each engorged peak. A sensation so strong shot through her that it frightened her and she tried to push Parker off of her.

"What?" He raised himself up on one elbow. Their gaze met as he tangled his fingers through her hair.

"I…" Cindy found herself at a loss for words. "I never—"

Parker's expression grew serious.

"You never *what?*"

"Felt like this. All these feelings and sensations, pushing around inside me, trying to find a way out. It's like…" She worried her lower lip.

"Like what?"

"It sounds silly."

"Nothing sounds silly if it's how you feel. Tell me."

"It's like I have to squash the feelings. Hold them

in. If I don't, if I let them break free, I'll be destroyed in the process. Shattered into a million pieces like Humpty-Dumpty. And all the king's horses and all the king's men won't be able to put me back together again.''

Parker captured her hand and pressed a quick, hot kiss to her palm. Then he placed her hand under his shirt, where she could feel the staccato beat of his heart.

"Like that? Like everything inside will just burst free and bring about destruction in the process?"

Cindy nodded, wide-eyed. How did he do that? How did he understand exactly how she felt when she didn't understand it herself?

"Do you believe those feelings can be released without destroying everything in their path?"

Cindy shook her head.

"What if I said I could prove it to you? Would you trust me to try?"

"I'm afraid," Cindy whispered. Hers was an admission tinged with guilt. With shame. Fear denoted weakness. She'd always been strong. She'd had to be.

"Have you been afraid before?"

She nodded, grateful he didn't dismiss or even diminish her fears.

"When?"

"All the time." She blanched. Where were these words coming from?

"And how do you combat the fear?"

"Run over it as if it doesn't exist."

"And then what?"

She couldn't believe they were even having this conversation. "It's like the wicked witch in the *Wizard of Oz*, after Dorothy poured water on her and she melted."

"Exactly," Parker said. "I want to make your fears melt away to nothing. Will you trust me to do that?"

"I hate being afraid." She didn't tell him why. The vulnerability. But he seemed to know, anyway.

"I know. Let me make it better."

Cindy drew in a deep, shuddery breath. "That means I have to trust you."

"It's easier than it sounds."

"I can't."

Parker kissed her lightly, coaxingly. "My grandmother always told me there's no such thing as 'can't.'"

"A wise woman, your grandmother."

"And determined."

Cindy swallowed deeply. Fear and excitement swept through her, causing her pulse to race and her heart to beat at what felt like triple-time. This must be the way bungee-jumpers feel just before they make the leap.

# Chapter Five

Cindy lay supine on the pillows and watched Parker roll to his feet. Where was he going? How could he move? She couldn't have budged if she'd had to. Her body felt weak and boneless and disassociated from her mind, a feeling that ought to have panicked her yet strangely didn't.

He made his way through the scattered pillows to the stereo and took his time inspecting her CD collection. As the soft subtle strains of "When a Man Loves a Woman" filled the room, Cindy felt herself sink ever more deeply into a surreal state of relaxation, almost as if someone else was controlling the signals to her brain. Parker disappeared into the kitchen and she heard water running. Maybe he was thirsty. Maybe he was already starting to regret the turn in their conversation. She had just managed to push herself to one elbow when he returned and knelt next to her. As he picked up one of her feet and started to massage it, Cindy realized that he had warmed a bowl of hand lotion from the bottle next to the sink.

Under his ministrations Cindy felt herself relax to near unconscious levels as he probed and stroked the tender, responsive cords and tendons in her foot and ankle. Sensually he slid his fingers between her toes and traced the outline of her instep. Cindy wouldn't have been surprised to learn she had sunk deep inside the pillows.

"Better?" Parker murmured. "No more volcanos threatening to erupt?"

"Mmm," Cindy murmured, too lethargic to move. She'd never felt so pampered in her life. His hands moved over her feet, stroking and kneading her leg past her calf to her knee. The sensations evoked by his touch were divine and Cindy shifted in an effort to signal her approval as her eyes drifted shut. All her feelings, all her responses, focused on Parker and the comfort of his touch.

He slid his fingers beneath her shorts. "These are in the way."

She had to agree. Clothing was an impediment, denying her the full benefits of his touch, and when he hooked his thumbs beneath her shorts and peeled them off she lifted her hips slightly in an effort to help.

The room temperature felt cool against her overheated skin as he continued to caress her. She felt nothing threatening or sexual in his touch, yet dormant sexual feelings were slowly being stirred to life. Cindy wriggled slightly. She felt a steady building of internal pressure, not frightening like earlier, but intensely pleasurable. The way a cat must feel when it's stroked in a particularly sensitive spot. If she was a cat she'd be purring loudly. The thought brought a smile to her lips.

This time when Parker touched her breasts she didn't jump in reaction but exhaled on a breathy moan of pleasure. He grazed her nipples with the palm of his hand in a barely there touch and the heat penetrated her skin like warm droplets of sunshine.

She was a flower slowly unfurling in the sunlight. Awash with heated sensation but much too languorous to move. All she could do was absorb everything she felt, pull it deep within her the way thirsty ground laps up rainfall. She'd been parched for far too long. And Parker seemed to intuitively know exactly what she needed. Exactly how she felt. Any excess would simply run right off of her. Drown her. Somehow he managed to lavish an exactly right amount of attention and care, one spot at a time before moving on.

She wasn't on fire. She wasn't afraid of being burned. Gloriously she felt herself come to life, awakening to the tactile sensations wrought by another's touch.

At some point Parker's lips replaced his fingertips. He laved her breasts, teased the nipples into rigid crests of delight that flooded pleasurable warmth to the juncture of her legs. Except it wasn't merely an internal warmth that snaked its way past her belly button, it was also Parker's lips and tongue pooling a wonderful trail of hot, wet delight.

Cindy's breath quickened to rise and fall in short, sharp bursts. A powerful sensation of building ten-

sions gathered within her. She felt as if she were bik-
ing uphill. Forcing all her energies to an unknown
summit. And just before she reached the finish line
there was Parker, his cheers providing her with that
last final surge.

Cindy screamed. Her body bucked with the power
of her release. And Parker placed one last, gentle kiss
to the woman part of her that throbbed and undulated
in the backwash of her ebbing tension.

He held her till the tremors subsided and her
breathing slowed back down to near normal. She felt
his large, capable hands on her head, smoothing the
damp tangle of hair back from her face.

"Nothing broken," Parker said. "I promised."

"Do you always keep your promises?"

"Believe it."

She touched his jaw, amazed by the fact that she
wasn't frightened or embarrassed or having any of the
feelings she might have expected.

"It's getting late." He cleared the dirty plates and
leftover Chinese food into the kitchen while Cindy
scrambled back into her clothes. Shifting her weight
from foot to foot she stood in the kitchen doorway as
he ran water in the sink and placed the food cartons
in the fridge. Surely he wasn't planning to hang
around and wash dishes?

He turned off the water, crossed the room and
dropped a light kiss on her forehead.

"'Night, Cinderella."

The door closed behind him with a muffled click.
Cindy stared through the window into the darkness

and wondered if there was any chance she had simply imagined the entire encounter. And what about that wretched shoe? She fell asleep dreaming about it above her in the clouds, clearly visible, frustratingly out of reach.

THE MINUTES POSITIVELY crawled past in the shoe store. Hilary blew in for a short time, but when Cindy mentioned going out of the shop during her lunch break, she suddenly had a pressing appointment at the theater, leaving Cindy stuck alone in the shop as usual.

Maybe Mr. Cheap would spell her when he came in to pick up the money and make his daily bank deposit.

"Mr. C.," she began when he arrived at his usual time. He'd started to smile as he thumbed through the stack of receipts, for business had been exceptionally good lately.

"No," he said, the smile fading so quickly it was as if she'd imagined it.

"You don't even know what I was going to say."

"Time off, a raise, a discount. Doesn't matter. It's still no."

Cindy took a breath. "You know that the labor relations code states a full-time worker is entitled to two fifteen-minute breaks and a half hour at lunch every day."

"So?"

"So everyone else is always at the theater for one reason or another. I never get those breaks."

"You don't want this job, plenty of others'll jump at the chance."

"That's not what I'm saying. If I could just—"

"No. Don't forget. Inventory next week."

Cindy gulped. She had to get that pump back into stock. "Believe me, I've hardly thought about anything else."

"Good. Good. What's your name again?"

They went through this every day. Howie Cecconni, affectionately known as Mr. Cheap, held to the theory that if he pretended not to know his staff by name, no one would feel secure enough to ask for a raise, let alone a day off.

"Cindy. It's Cindy, Mr. C."

"Right, Mindy," he mumbled, gathering up the money and credit card imprints. "Hold down the fort while I'm gone. Let's have another bonanza day."

He held the door open for two customers on their way in, even doffed his hat and made small talk to the women about the weather. Cindy shook her head upon hearing his parting shot about how "Mindy will take good care of you both."

Both of the women were not much older than Cindy, but had that air of Madronna Beach money about them. Usually it was the newly monied who put on the airs.

"We'll let you know if we need help," one of the women said with a dismissive wave in Cindy's direction.

Cindy went back to rearranging the front window of the shop. In no way did she intentionally eavesdrop, but it was impossible not to overhear the conversation between the pair, who made no effort to lower their voices.

"What are you wearing to the wedding?"

"Well, I decided it was a perfect excuse to buy that new Betsey Johnson that's been simply calling to me this past week. Of course, Bruce feels differently." Her friend let out a knowing laugh. "What about you?"

"I already have something new that's been begging for an excuse for an outing." The two giggled childishly, and then sobered.

"And you'll never believe who I just heard is planning to make an appearance."

"Who?"

"None other than her royal pain herself, Tammy."

"No!" The other one gasped, as if this was the most monstrous development.

"Yes. Poor Parker. I wonder if he knows."

"Someone should tell him."

"Someone ought to tell Lisa. Let her break the news."

"See any shoes crying to be yours?"

"Not really. You?"

"No. I am parched, though. I fancy a nice dry martini."

"Sounds like a plan."

The bell tinkled as the duo left, and Cindy eased down off of the stepladder in the front window. She'd felt frozen up there, afraid to move and miss a word of the conversation.

She wondered whose upcoming wedding had everyone so stirred up. One thing she did know. Tammy had to be the one who'd broken Parker's heart all those years ago. What were the odds she was coming back hoping for a second chance?

Finally six o'clock rolled around and Cindy could close and lock the shop. Hopping onto her bike, she pedaled out to Mr. Hubble's weed-choked mansion as fast as her legs would carry her. Surely she could reason with the old boy, perhaps explain the significance of the shoe. She knew he was unpredictable, and was still reeling from having glimpsed this other side of him. Who would have guessed that eccentric exterior masked the soul of a poet? A die-hard romantic who believed his soul mate was still out there · for him.

Goodness knew she and Marissa had debated the point time and again, both agreeing to disagree. Marissa, in spite of everything that had happened in her life, still believed in the happily-ever-after stuff of bedtime stories. Good triumphant over evil. Knights on white chargers slaying fire-breathing dragons. Fairy godmothers. Was she the only one in town who didn't harbor any such nonsensical belief?

Hubble's mansion had been built late in the 1800s by one of the first families to permanently settle in the beach area. The gardens, now irreparably overgrown, must have been beautiful way back when. The house was massive, three stories high, stunting its neighbors. She'd heard rumors Hubble only occupied the first floor and gave the other two floors over to his cats. The creatures were everywhere. They had taken over the front steps, the porch, the garden; there were even several sunning themselves on the roof above the porch. They greeted her noisily as she made her way up the front steps, avoiding the hazards of paws and tails, and lifted the tarnished lion's head knocker. She could hear the hollow echo of the knocker through the house, but no one answered the door.

"He's gone away, love."

Cindy whirled. An enormously fat woman in a loose muumuu-type gown leaned over the fence, which was so rickety, Cindy was half afraid it might collapse from the weight. In startling contrast to Hubble's jungle, the woman's cottage-style home was tiny and well kept, the yard immaculate.

"Gone? Where? For how long?"

"Don't know for sure. All I know is he asked me to feed the cats till he got back."

"Thanks." Dejectedly, Cindy pushed her way past the cats and kittens, back to her bike. "If you see him, would you tell him that Cindy stopped by?"

"Right-o, dolly. He don't get much company. Neither of us does. Would you care to stop in for a cup of tea with Maude?"

Tea with a lonely old lady was the last thing in the world she wanted, but one look at the woman's hopeful face and Cindy couldn't find it in her heart to reject the offer of kindness. Maybe because kindness seemed to be a rare commodity in her life.

Actually, Parker had never been anything but kind

and she'd been churlish and small to him. She vowed then and there to be nicer to Parker. If she ever saw him again, that was.

The house was as tidy inside as out, if a little cluttered for Cindy's tastes.

"You'd be Sheri's girl, then," Maude stated matter-of-factly as she poured fragrant Earl Grey from a beautifully crafted pottery pot into matching cups with saucers. She pushed a cream and sugar set toward a flabbergasted Cindy.

"How did you know that?"

"If you aren't the image of Sheri when she was your age," the woman said. "Except I'm thinking you've got your father's eyes."

Cindy blanched. "You knew my father?" The topic had been taboo with her mother from the day she was old enough to ask until finally she'd got smart enough to stop asking, half afraid Sheri didn't say because Sheri didn't know.

"Lordy, yes. So in love the pair of them. Did a body good just to see them together. Made a soul believe in love again." Her enormous bosom heaved as she sighed a fluttery sigh. "Sam and Sheri. Such a tragedy."

Cindy took a sip of tea, then set her cup down carefully. "This is my mother's pottery."

Maude nodded, as if it were the most natural thing in the world. "I knitted your first wee pair of booties, I did."

"What happened to my father?" She couldn't yet

bring herself to even say his name. Sam. It felt too weird after all this time to have a name for him.

"People said they were too young to know their own minds, of course. That's how people were back then. Shaking their heads and saying "I told you so" once it was obvious you'd got started. Sam was a migrant farmworker, which is how they met, out picking in the fields. With you on the way he wanted to make better money, to provide for the two of you. So he went out on a commercial fishing vessel. Swore he'd be back before you were born. Sheri, of course, begged him not to go." She heaved a huge sigh that set her bosoms and chins aquiver in tandem. "Freak storm broke out at sea. Every one on board was drowned. And your grandparents, God rest their souls, refused to condone Sheri keeping you. Thought she was too irresponsible, but she proved them wrong. I know she was a wild child and all, but she's always had a pure heart."

"She never told me about my father. Eventually I stopped asking."

"The loss cut her deep, poor girl. And there are those of us who, having had that one great love, refuse to make do ever again."

"Refuse to make do?" Cindy said. "Do you know how many boyfriends she's had over the years? I doubt she can even count that high."

Maude set down her cup and leaned toward Cindy across the table, her chins wobbling. "None she ever gave custody of her heart to, I'd wager. That's why they didn't last. Sheri was young. Took her solace in other men.'' She slapped her considerable girth. ''Me, as you can plainly see, took the solace of my loss in food. Other folks might bury themselves in work. Or drink. Anything to try and ease the pain.''

So, Cindy mused as she pedaled her way back to town, Parker, who had lost his one true love, had buried himself in work. And in trying to make himself feel useful by helping others. It all made perfectly good sense to her now. It wasn't till she reached her apartment that she recalled just why she'd gone out to Hubble's in the first place. She still hadn't retrieved that blasted red pump. The message light was blinking on her answering machine. Parker. She rewound the tape, knowing she couldn't deal with talking to him right now. Marissa, though. Marissa would lend a sympathetic ear. She got back on her bike and pedaled to her friend's house.

Except something was off there, as well. She glanced at her best friend, who was staring into space, wearing an expression Cindy had never seen before. Marissa had always been a beauty, yet she appeared different today. Soft and glowy and…kind of lit up from the inside out.

Cindy grabbed a chair, spun it around and straddled it, her face on a level with Marissa's.

''Spill!'' she demanded. ''Out with it!''

Marissa returned to the present with a blink and a jerk. ''I beg your pardon?''

''You can't fool me, girlfriend. Something's up.''

''Oh, Cindy.'' Marissa exhaled her name. ''I met the most incredible man. Gentle, soft-spoken. Shy, I think. He talked to me. Treated me…'' She sighed, her hands fluttering in her lap.

Cindy felt instantly ashamed. She'd been so focused on herself, her stuff, and here was Marissa, dying to share, and she was almost too self-involved to even notice. Some friend she was!

''He treated you how, Rissa. Where did the two of you meet?''

''I was at the stables. I was riding Cappuccino.''

Oh, great, Cindy thought. Some guy chatted Marissa up, not realizing that she spent ninety-nine percent of her time in a wheelchair. Cindy's protective instincts rose to the fore. She couldn't bear the thought of her friend being hurt.

''There was an accident. I fell off.''

''Marissa! Are you okay?''

''Unhurt, luckily. But I had the wind knocked out of me. He was so kind. So solicitous. He treated me no differently from anyone else. Even after I told him the reason I couldn't get up.''

''Humph,'' Cindy said.

''He was really quite lovely,'' Marissa said. ''He was there tending one of the mares whose foal was breech.''

Cindy sat up straight. ''A vet? This fellow you met was a vet?''

''That's what Ruth said. All I know is that he had the most amazing soft gray eyes. Eyes far too old for his face.''

''How old was this guy? Did you happen to get his name?''

"Tom," Marissa said dreamily. "His name was Tom."

"Tom, you say?" Cindy echoed. What a small world! Since tomorrow was Sunday, she'd just take a little mosey out to Tom's compound, Cindy decided, and reassure herself that his intentions toward her friend were honorable.

Except when she arrived the next day, Tom was nowhere in sight. And as she chewed on her frustration by tackling a dirty cage, who should drive in but Parker. Now she hardly knew what to think. It felt like she was a bit player in a bizarre Shakespearean comedy. A midsummer's day's compound.

Maybe Parker hadn't come looking for her. Maybe he'd come to see Tom. Whatever his motivation, he caught her attention immediately by waving a bright red shoe in front of her, the sight of which sent her flying gratefully into his arms.

"Parker! The Louboutin!" She checked it over as carefully as a mother counts her newborn's fingers and toes, relieved to find it in pristine condition. "Where? How?"

"From Hubble. Where else?"

"But I was there yesterday. Maude, his next door neighbor, told me he'd left town."

"Luckily I caught him before he left. I know you told me not to interfere, but...." He shrugged, looked down at his feet and went into his irresistible little-boy-with-his-hand-in-the-cookie-jar-but-who-could-stay-mad-at-him routine.

Not Cindy. She was too relieved to have the shoe

back in her possession. "You enjoy the white-knight-to-the-rescue role, don't you?"

"Guilty as charged. And now I'm kind of hoping you'll do something for me."

Here it comes. The catch. "And just what might that be?"

"I've got a wedding to attend next weekend. Would you do me the honor of being my date for the event?"

*The wedding!*

"You don't want to take me."

She was hot, sweaty, tired, and refused to believe anyone would deliberately choose to be seen with her, given the way she looked at that particular moment.

Parker just leaned against the row of cages she was cleaning and flashed her a smile that melted her insides, damn him. "I wouldn't ask you if I didn't want you."

"I'm not—"

"Not what?"

She recalled the duo in the shoe store. The fact that Parker's one true love would be on the scene. He needed someone of his own pedigree on his arm.

"I don't fit in with those society types."

"They put their pants on one leg at a time, same as anyone," Parker said. "Cindy." Damn, but he proved hard to resist. Those serious ocean-blue eyes shimmered irresistibly at her. "I don't feel comfortable showing up unescorted."

"All right," she said flatly. "I'll do it. But only

because you helped me move and get the shoe back. After that we're even.''

A sudden storm blew through those compelling eyes. She focused instead on the way a muscle twitched in his jaw. ''No.''

''No?'' Cindy couldn't believe she'd heard him right. ''Didn't you hear? I said I'd go with you.''

''I don't want you as my date due to some misplaced idea of a big debit card in the sky you want to see a zero balance on.''

Naturally, the minute he turned her down Cindy started to obsess. Parker had been nothing but kind and helpful to her, while she in turn had been churlish and small-minded. Not to mention selfish. Shockingly selfish.

She'd immediately set her sights to have Parker change his mind, even going so far as to enlist Tom's help once he appeared. And when finally Parker capitulated, with what appeared to be the utmost reluctance, she was left with the disturbing sense that she had been masterfully set up and reeled in.

But at least she would no longer be beholden to him. The wedding was on the upcoming weekend, an event that threw her into a complete tizzy about her wardrobe.

Marissa, as usual, came to the rescue, arriving the next day with a pile of fashion magazines. She pawed through Cindy's meager wardrobe and finally decided on a vintage port-colored velvet dress.

''I'll roast,'' Cindy said. ''That's why I never wear it. It's too hot.''

"I'll take the sleeves right off," Marissa said. "Then I'll lower the neckline and raise the hem."

"By the weekend?"

"By the weekend," Marissa said. "I think it's great that you're going out with Parker. I really like him."

"I'm not going out with him. He just doesn't want to go to this wedding alone. Can't say as how I blame him." She'd never told Marissa about what had happened between her and Parker the night she met Hubble. In fact, she'd done her darnedest to forget all about it. But every once in a while her fickle memory would get the best of her. She'd see a bottle of Heineken beer. Or catch a whiff of Chinese food. Her body would suddenly be assaulted with a flood of remembered sensations and tingles. How she hated the vivid exactness of her memory.

"Quit fidgeting," Marissa said around a mouthful of pins. Cindy stood between her friend and a full-length mirror in a half-picked-apart dress and watched as Marissa nipped and tucked and snipped.

"Sorry," Cindy said as she tried her hardest to stand still. She settled for sticking out her tongue at her reflection. She hated getting dressed up.

"Who's getting married?"

"One of Parker's old girlfriends, Bambi somebody."

"There's a somebody named Bambi? In this town?" Marissa smothered a giggle. "And you and Parker are going to her wedding?"

"Apparently he stays on very good terms with anyone he's ever been involved with."

*Even me,* she thought. But she didn't say it out loud. Because they hadn't been involved. Not past that one night, anyway. Not like Parker and Little Miss Gymnast-who-broke-his-heart, Tammy.

# Chapter Six

Cindy gave herself one final glance in the mirror, determined it would be the last. She'd given up on her hair, along with the bag stuffed full of cosmetics that Marissa had forced on her. She had agreed, with the utmost reluctance, to accept a pair of seamed black stockings and the most outrageous high-heeled sandals she had ever worn.

Marissa had arrived to watch her get ready, and even she had agreed that the touch of mascara and the port-colored lipstick were adornment enough.

Damp-palmed Cindy paced the length of her apartment. She couldn't even shift the blame to Parker for talking her into this. It had been all her own doing.

She heard him pull up out back and was out the door and halfway across the parking lot by the time he had stepped out of a black Mustang convertible. She stopped short. "Where's your truck?"

"Tucked in for the night." He just gave her an admiring top-to-toe perusal. "You look fantastic. Just try not to look quite so much like you're ready to face the firing squad. My parents aren't all that bad."

If Cindy wasn't already rooted to the spot, his words would have had that effect. "Your mother and father? You didn't tell me they'd be there."

"They're Bambi's godparents. Did I forget to mention that?" Parker's tone was a sight too innocent as he opened the passenger door and waited patiently for her to regain control of her uncooperative limbs.

Cindy got herself in hand and sailed forth with all the regal bearing she could manage in those ridiculous shoes. After settling her in, Parker seated himself behind the wheel and gave her an engaging grin that was almost impossible not to respond to. Cindy managed.

"Anything else you neglected to mention?" She was proud of the tiny bit of frost she managed to inject into her words. "You and I giving the toast to the bride?"

"Nothing I can think of, offhand."

As they neared the golf club Parker snuck a sideways glance at his silent passenger and wondered what it might take to get her to loosen up. He wanted her to have fun tonight, to prove to her that they could have fun together in spite of her feelings about class differences and everything else that she choked on around him.

The driveway was lined by huge palm trees, and as he pulled up under the porte cochere he studied the club's facade, trying to see it through Cindy's eyes. Was it the earthbound equivalency of a spaceship, ready to transport her to another planet?

For him the club was an environment that was as

natural as breathing. Something that had always been there, a part of his life.

The parking attendant sprang forward, opened the passenger door and helped Cindy alight. Parker didn't like the way the guy's eyes lingered on Cindy's legs.

"Here." He barged between them and passed his keys to the man, who was still grinning foolishly, as if he'd never seen a female before. A safe bet the guy had never seen one quite like Cindy. He took her arm and turned her to where bright lights spilled through the entranceway. Despite the fragrant warmth of the night air, Cindy's skin felt icy cold beneath his fingers.

"Loosen up." He spoke directly in her ear, unable to resist flicking the delicate shell shape with the tip of his tongue. He felt a shiver chase through her. "They're not that bad."

"When you're used to having a serving tray in your hand, you tend to feel quite naked without one." Cindy softened her words with a smile.

"Well you don't look naked. And as long as that dress doesn't disappear at midnight, you'll be fine." He gave her hand a reassuring squeeze as they passed through the open doorway and up the wide tile stairway toward the Grande Salon. Twinkling white lights outlined each stair tread, and twined the handrail.

"Remind me not to catch the bouquet," Cindy mumbled as they passed more than a dozen huge wicker baskets dripping with fresh flowers, cluttering the hallway.

"Bambi and Chet eloped last month, much to her

parents' disgust. They got married on the beach at Baja. Tonight is just a little gig her folks insisted on throwing for their closest friends.''

''Little gig,'' Cindy echoed as they reached the salon entrance and paused.

Parker shrugged. ''Just three or four hundred of their nearest and dearest friends and hangers-on.'' He kept a firm hold of her elbow, half afraid she might turn tail and run. Although Cindy was tougher than she looked, Parker knew she wasn't half so tough as she pretended.

The Grande Salon was a fairyland of twinkling lights wound through some sort of fake twisted branches, which were stuck in terra-cotta pots and scattered all around the room. Probably something Bambi's mom had seen in a Martha Stewart magazine and decided to copy. It made an interesting effect, albeit too much for Parker's tastes. He felt as if he had landed in the middle of a Disneyland attraction. Any moment now he expected to hear the orchestra strike up ''It's a Small World....''

The shindig was already well under way. He and Cindy stood just inside the doorway, he giving her time to get her bearings. Hell, get his own bearings was more like it. Just because he had grown up in this milieu didn't mean he had to like it.

He flagged down a server hastening past with a tray of champagne and passed one to Cindy. ''This might help to take the edge off.''

''I'm not much of a drinker,'' Cindy said doubtfully, tossing her head back and draining her glass in a single swallow.

Parker laughed out loud.

"What?" She sounded insulted by his laughter, which he had meant as a compliment.

He gave her a close hug. "You. You are so damn refreshing in my life."

All of a sudden he felt her stiffen. She turned to ice in his arms. "Hey, what did I say?"

But Cindy seemed unaware of him. All her attention was riveted on the man bearing hard toward them. He saw her catch herself, visibly saw her force herself to relax.

"Davis," the other man greeted him. "And none other than our own little Cinderella."

"Lowther," Parker responded, also responding to the stab of jealousy running through him. Clearly Lowther was acquainted with Cindy. And she was hardly immune to his presence.

"Hello, Brad," she said quietly.

Parker felt like growling territorially when the other man reached out and trailed a finger along Cindy's bare arm. "It's been too long, Cinderella. Promise you'll save me a dance later."

"I make no promises. You know that."

"I remember."

After one last, very obvious leer in her direction, Brad Lowther turned, stuffed his hands in his pockets and sauntered away, whistling tunelessly.

"Where do you know him from?" Parker asked.

"We went out a few times," Cindy said, with what Parker perceived to be forced casualness.

"Only a few times?" He couldn't fathom this possessive streak of jealousy, it was new for him.

"Very few times," Cindy said. But her lips were still colorless and she had goose bumps on her bare arms, despite the warm room and the crush of bodies around them.

"Guy's a goof," Parker said gruffly, wishing it was just the two of them alone someplace, anyplace but here.

"That's a polite way of putting it."

Cindy's words warmed him right to the core. Clearly she had no use for Lowther and the man's belief that he was, and always had been, God's gift to women.

Parker continued to be surprised by the number of people who stopped and greeted Cindy by name. In mere minutes she started to lose that tense, rigid look and actually appeared as if she might relax and enjoy herself.

"How do you know all these people?" he asked as Cindy introduced him yet again to someone he didn't know.

She slanted him a sideways look. "Madronna Beach is a small town. And I'm not quite the hermit you seem to think I am."

"Drink this one slower," Parker said as he passed her a second glass of champagne, adding admiringly, "And yet another side to the girl called Cinderella."

"I've yet to ride in a pumpkin," she said.

"I'm sure it can be arranged." He placed one hand on the small of her back and steered her across the room, aware he could happily leave his hand there, enjoying the way the warmth of her skin seeped through the richness of her velvet dress. "Let's go see my folks."

"How lovely to see you again, Cindy," said Parker's mother, Robin, as warm and sincere as Cindy recalled from their last meeting. "How beautiful you look." Recalling how she had been on her less-than-best behaviour at the time, Cindy was grateful for the chance to make a better second impression.

"It was awfully nice of Parker to invite me," she said. "Usually I'm on the other side of the serving table at these events."

"Jan said that exact same thing," Robin said, turning and including an older version of Parker into the conversation. "Have you met my husband, Gord?"

"It's a pleasure."

Gord Davis, like Parker, met her gaze with that impetuous boyish twinkle, underscored by an enchanting air of seriousness.

"My pleasure," Gord corrected her, squeezing her hand between both of his. "I have a few expectant patients, but I entreated them to hold off at least until tomorrow. Not that they looked happy with the idea."

"Can you blame them, darling? Oh, here comes Lisa. Cindy, you must meet our daughter. She simply adores the shoes you picked out for her. I know she wants to thank you in person."

"It was all Parker's doing, really. I had very little—"

"Nonsense. Parker knows less about women's footwear than I know about trucks."

Gord chortled. "Lisa is our goddess of shoes, always has been. Her Barbie dolls might have been seldom clothed, but never did they go barefoot."

A rangy brunette joined them, hugged her mother, pressed a kiss to Gord's cheek and draped herself over Parker. "I'm Lisa," she said, extending one foot to display the strappy multicolored Mancini. "I know for a fact my reputation has preceded me." Her smile was infectious.

"I'm Cindy."

"You have wonderful taste in shoes, Cindy. I like the ones you're wearing."

Cindy felt her whole face crease in a smile. "I expected someone in medical school would be militant on the evils of stiletto heels."

"Well, a girl can hardly work in them, but they have their place." She gave the group a bawdy wink. "I blame Dad, really. Anything he told me was bad for me, I automatically wanted duplicates of."

Gord shrugged, looking not at all unhappy with the direction of the conversation. "What's a poor father to do?"

Lisa turned to Parker. "I guess you heard Tammy is on the guest list for the evening's festivities?"

"I hadn't heard," Parker said.

"Forewarned is forearmed," Lisa replied.

Cindy noticed the trace of concern cross Robin's

face. Clearly Robin was worried Parker still had feelings for his one true love, his high school sweetheart, and how he might react upon seeing her again.

"What makes you think I need warning or arming?" Parker asked.

"I know what she's like. If she came back here with a definite purpose in mind such as—"

Robin interrupted smoothly. "I don't think we ought to bore Cindy with that old history, do you, dear?"

"Cindy ought to be prepared, too. If some wiry little redhead shows up and tries to strongarm Parker away from her—"

"Lisa…" No mistaking the warning in Gord's tone.

"Listen, everyone, I appreciate your concern," Parker said. "But this is getting out of hand. It's Bambi's big night. Focus on that."

"Am I interrupting?" Cindy could have hugged Jan for her timely appearance, but Lisa beat her to it. As she and Jan squealed and hugged and reminisced, Cindy was reminded one more time of her outsider's status. Even though she was friends with Jan, she was also Jan's employee. She hadn't gone to school with these girls. Hadn't shared their history.

As the small talk escalated and Cindy felt more and more isolated, she glanced over at Parker. Something in his gaze told her he knew exactly how she felt.

Damn, she looked so lost and vulnerable, like a little girl all dressed up with no place to go. Abruptly he made their excuses and whisked Cindy away, unable to credit the surge of possessiveness that swept through him. He wished everyone else in the room would just disappear and leave them alone. He wanted her all to himself, he realized with a start. They had barely arrived and already he was tired of sharing her.

"That dress of yours has to be some kind of lethal weapon," Parker said. The great thing about Cindy was how totally unaffected she was. She had no idea just how attractive she really was, a refreshing change from girls Parker knew who unabashedly exploited their looks and connections to achieve their own ends.

"This old thing?" Cindy punctuated her words with a tinkle of laughter that penetrated every hungry fiber of his being. "I like your parents," she said. "They seem so genuine."

Parker pulled his attention from admiring Cindy and feeling damn lucky to be the one here with her, to focus on what she was saying.

"I've met my share of phonies in my day. I have no use for them."

"Speaking of phonies." Parker spun her around so she could see the head table. "Bambi's father is drunk. He's about to get a royal chew-out from Bambi's mother. Chet's parents are on the other side of the happy couple, pretending to be deaf. See them?"

"The mother looks like she could enjoy chewing glass."

"How'd you get to be such an astute judge of people?"

"Most people aren't that hard to read. Except, of course, for you."

"Me?" Parker pretended to be hurt. "I'm an open book."

"Maybe for someone who reads braille," Cindy said. "Answer me this. Why did you bring me here tonight? And forget the 'didn't want to come alone' part. That's rubbish."

"I think…" Parker paused. "I guess I wanted to prove to you that you could be comfortable in my world."

Cindy nodded sagely. "That's exactly what I thought. And you know what? Therein lies the problem."

"Problem? What problem?"

"You really do think of it that way, that I'm an alien being, uncertain about penetrating this safe, secure, stuffy world of yours. There's one world, Parker. One set of inhabitants."

"You're the one who said you aren't comfortable around the society folks. Your words, not mine."

"That was my way of trying to let you down easy. To tell you what you expected to hear."

"Are you sorry you came?"

"Of course not," Cindy said, a little too vehemently for Parker's liking. "How could I be sorry? It's clearly the social event of the season."

"I wish we were alone someplace."

Cindy drew back to study him. "Why alone?"

"Because I wouldn't have to be constantly ducking Lowther and guys like him who'll try to take you away." She did it again. Turned into a Popsicle in his arms. He pulled her onto the balcony into the softly scented night air. "What gives?"

She wrapped her arms protectively around her mid-section. "What do you mean?"

"You and Lowther. I never liked the guy. What'd he try and pull?"

"Apparently the word 'no' isn't in his vocabulary," Cindy said at last.

"He forced himself on you?" Parker felt his hands close into fists.

"We were down on the beach by the pier. Jules heard me and helped convince him that 'no' truly does mean no. He made some unflattering remarks about my parentage and white trash upbringing. I vowed then and there to stay away from society-type boys."

"I wish I'd known," Parker said.

"What difference would it have made?"

"I didn't take no for an answer, either," Parker said. "Selfishly I wanted you with me tonight. I was fully prepared to do whatever it took."

"You society boys are all cut from the same cloth in that regard," Cindy said. "Accustomed to getting what you want."

"Not me," Parker said. "What I wanted eluded me, and it still does."

*Tammy,* Cindy thought. His one true love, due to put in an appearance here tonight. No sooner did the thought make itself heard, than it was followed by the voice.

"I wondered where y'all have been hiding yourself, Parker." The voice was low and sexy. Almost a purr. Matched by the graceful feline movement of the petite redhead who sashayed, there was no other word for it, in their direction.

Cindy felt tall and gawky and awkward. Parker stared as if in a trance. Cindy slunk back into the shadows, where she watched in horror and fascination as Tammy wound her limbs around Parker and gave him a long, slow, intimate kiss. One he made no show of ending anytime soon.

Keeping her arm linked with Parker's, Tammy turned to Cindy, dispelling Cindy's belief that the girl hadn't even seen her. "I hope you don't mind. Parker and I go way back. Way, way back. I'm Tammy."

*And he's mine,* she might as well have added.

"I've heard about you," Cindy said.

"From Parker?" she asked with a coquettish smile.

"Lisa mentioned you'd be here tonight."

The smile turned into a pout.

"Lisa! No one will ever be good enough for her big brother. Or has she changed, Parker? Mellowed in her old age?"

"Why don't you go see for yourself?" Parker worked his arm free and took a step toward Cindy.

Tammy stepped between them. "I like what I see right here."

Cindy held her ground. The next move was Parker's.

"Good to see you again, Tammy. I think it's time we went and found our seats." He claimed Cindy and ushered her back inside. She knew Tammy's presence had had an effect on him but didn't know him well enough to judge if the effect was good or bad.

"Do you still love her?"

"Where'd that come from?"

"Someone recently extolled the virtues of being direct."

"I didn't realize you were paying such close attention." He took his time before he answered. "I loved her very much at one time. I wanted to be just like my folks. Get married and live happily ever after."

"And what happened? Her career?"

"In a way it was worse. She started using drugs."

"Drugs?"

"To enhance her performance. I'm a doctor's son. I knew, long-term, the negative effects. I tried everything I could to get her off them. Nothing worked. We fought. She left town. I felt bad for a long, long time."

"Losing the girl or losing the dream?"

"Both, I suppose."

"It's not too late to have them both."

"It's too late for me and Tammy."

Not if Miss Tammy has her way, Cindy thought.

Their conversation came to a natural end as the meal was served, and her attention was claimed by the woman on her other side, a Glass Slipper customer. As soon as the plates were cleared Cindy stood and excused herself to go powder her nose.

"Hurry back." Parker made a little-boy face. "I hardly had a chance to talk to you."

Parker sat twirling the bowl of his spoon around on the crisply ironed tablecloth and glanced to his parents at the other end of the table. It had thrown him off seeing Tammy tonight, but only for a minute. Cindy was so damn perceptive. It hadn't been the loss of the girl so much as the loss of his dreams.

He'd started a mindless round of dating nearly every girl in town until one morning he'd woken up next to a warm and willing female whose name he couldn't remember. Enough of that!

Work had claimed his full attention right up until recently, when he'd walked into that damn shoe store and seen Cindy inching her way down the ladder. Something inside of him came to life in her presence. Something that stirred the ashes of his own belief for happiness.

So where was his date, anyway? He suffered through the usual barrage of boring wedding toasts and speeches, way too conscious of the empty chair next to him and how much time had passed since she had excused herself. She'd seemed to be having a good time. She wouldn't have ducked out on him. Would she? Maybe that recent scene with Tammy had proved too much for her.

Parker scoured the Grande Salon, trying not to panic. This was a safe neighborhood. A secure club. No chance Cindy had been accosted and spirited away someplace. Lowther was still here, no doubt preying on some other hapless victim. At least he wasn't going after Cindy.

After a fruitless search, some unnamed instinct

caused him to follow one of the black-and-white-garbed wait people into the kitchen. Cindy stood in front of the sink, her back to him, swathed in an enormous starched white apron that appeared to be wrapped around her twice. The only recognizable part of her was the lower half of her legs, unmistakable in those sexy seamed black stockings and high heels.

"What are you doing?"

"Parker." She turned around, her hands encased in oversize orange rubber gloves. "I'm almost done. I was just about to come back and find you."

"You are a guest here, not one of the help." As he spoke Parker fumbled with the knot on her apron, trying to rip the goddamn thing off her. He gave up and swore loudly. Cindy's eyes widened.

"What? You think I didn't feel comfortable out there? That I felt better-suited in here among the working class?" Her eyes blazed furiously into his. "You, Parker Davis, are a dreadful snob. For your information there was an accident. One of the girls slipped on some water and broke her ankle. Bambi's mother was hysterical over the delay it might cause. Half a dozen of us came in to lend a hand rinsing the dishes and loading the dishwasher. No different from anything I'd do as a guest in someone's house." As she spoke she peeled off the gloves and apron and threw them at him. "Trust you to jump to the totally wrong conclusion!" She turned him around and pushed him up in front of a wall-mounted mirror. "Take a good look, Parker. Like what you see?"

With that she turned on her heel and stalked from the kitchen.

Left staring into the mirror, Parker had to admit he didn't care for what he saw. Not one bit. He was everything Cindy accused him of. And more.

# Chapter Seven

Cindy felt fury reverberate through each angry stride that carried her through the Grande Salon, down the tile staircase and out into the star-studded night air.

"Which car, ma'am?" asked the same goofy-grinned attendant.

Cindy had fully intended to have him call her a cab. Abruptly she changed her mind. "The black Mustang convertible, please."

Guiltily she glanced over her shoulder, half expecting to see Parker thunder down the stairs toward her as headlights cut through the darkness, fueled by the throaty five-liter engine. As the car grumbled to a halt inches away Cindy fumbled in her bag for a tip for the attendant, then slid behind the wheel.

She scanned the lighted instrument panel, which appeared to have more dials than a 747 cockpit. Manual transmission. It had been a while since she'd used a clutch, but surely it was like riding a bike.

"Slide over." She glanced up. Parker stood at her elbow. When she didn't move he opened the door. "Slide over. I'll take you home."

She couldn't move. She felt frozen into place. After a long, silent minute that felt like a hundred, Parker shut the door, walked around the car and got in the passenger side. "Okay, then. You drive."

"Really?"

"Why not?"

"I'm out of practice."

Parker shrugged. "I'm out of practice at apologies. But you're right. I looked in that mirror tonight and I didn't like who I saw staring back."

Carefully Cindy put in the clutch and eased her other foot onto the gas. Her confidence grew as she shifted gears smoothly and felt the powerful car leap forward, as impatient as she was to be under way. Overhead the velvet-cloaked sky was speckled with stars. The air was warm and sultry with just a faint hint of danger. Or was that merely the way Cindy felt? About to embark on something new and exciting.

She drove through town and continued north along the winding coast highway, where they had the road and the night all to themselves. Nothing except guardrails stood between the Mustang, the jagged cliffs and the ever-changing Pacific shoreline. Abruptly Cindy pulled in at the lookout and turned off the engine and the lights. The night air wrapped her safe and comfortable in its cocoon.

"That's better." She rested her head against the seat back, closed her eyes and drank in the sound of the breakers hitting the cliff, the salt-tinged seaweed smell that signaled home to her.

"What's better?" She heard Parker slide closer. His fingertips brushed her bare shoulder, a light caress that didn't feel like an accident.

"I couldn't hear the ocean before."

"Sorry about dragging you into that ordeal back there. And about jumping to conclusions."

"It wasn't all that bad. Face your demons?"

She could sense his grin. "You mean ghosts of girlfriends past? I think my family was way more worried than I was."

"She meant a lot to you once."

"Believe it or not, it was actually very freeing to see her again. I can let go of the guilt."

"You felt guilty?"

"Of course I did. That I couldn't love her enough, be enough for her to keep her clean. Like she was broken and I couldn't fix her. At least in teenage idealistic terms."

"You tried."

"I tried way too hard. And I'm afraid, if she hadn't left, I'd still be trying. We would have destroyed each other."

"Judging by her behaviour tonight, I'd say she's more than willing to give you another chance."

"One thing I did learn from it is that you can't go back. Gotta keep moving forward. Cindy?"

She felt him drawing closer. He was getting ready to kiss her. She just knew it. Abruptly she leaned forward, turned the key and threw the car into Reverse. "Speaking of moving forward."

"Any particular place in mind?"

"Not much farther. Why?" She flashed him a teasing grin. "You hoping we run out of gas?"

"I haven't done that since high school. And at the time I found it didn't help improve my odds any with the girl. Sure did get her father riled, though."

They traveled a few more miles before Cindy spotted the rutted, overgrown dirt driveway. It had been years since she'd been out this way and she almost missed it in the dark. Around the bend she stopped and left the motor idling. Barely visible by the headlights' glow was a shadowy ragtag collection of tents, sheds and outbuildings. Not far away a generator hummed noisily, audible over the car's engine. A dog's bark echoed through the night air.

"This is it, huh? The place you grew up?"

"This is it."

"You going in?"

Cindy shook her head. "You said it yourself. You can't go back. When I left, I was mad at my mother. I swore I'd never be back. That the next move had to come from her."

"Why were you mad at her?"

"I forget how old I was when I figured out she wasn't like other mothers, but her being different meant I was different. No kid likes standing out from the others. Anyway, this was home." She turned toward Parker. "It looks smaller than I remembered, a little more run-down."

Parker didn't say anything. She wondered what he was thinking.

"Funny thing, I know I was happy here. Lots of

people lived here back then. As the only kid I got lots of attention and had lots of freedom. For a long time I didn't know my life was that much different from anyone else's.''

"Sounds pretty laid-back.''

"It was. And tonight, at that fancy gig of yours, I realized no one else in the room had anything close to the kind of upbringing I had.''

"One of the many things that makes you unique.''

"Your turn to drive.'' Cindy opened the door and got out and Parker did likewise, sliding behind the wheel. Cindy stood in front of the car, just looking, a barrage of poignant emotions churning around inside of her. Childhood memories both happy and sad.

The Mustang idled behind her but she couldn't bring herself to get back into it. Dirt and gravel crunched underfoot, cushioned by weeds. She took a deep breath of air, redolent of sun-warmed soil and dried grasses. Out of the gloom she saw the silhouette of a man approaching, a large dark-coated dog at his side. The dog broke free and raced up to her, wagging its tale.

"Hello, Blue.'' Behind her, Parker cut the engine but left the headlights on, enough to illuminate the poker-faced features of the slim, pony-tailed man. When Parker reached Cindy's side Blue growled low in his throat.

"Anyone but you, Cindy, Blue'd a been barking his head off.''

"Hello, Frank. I'm just glad he remembers me. This is my friend, Parker. Be good, Blue. He's okay.''

Blue sniffed Parker thoroughly and seemed to agree with her judgment.

Frank was just as Cindy recalled. A man of few words.

"Place hasn't changed much through the years," Cindy offered.

"Nope," Frank said.

"I'm glad you're still... That Sheri isn't alone."

Frank nodded.

"I just, um, wanted to show Parker where I grew up."

"Sheri's over in the meditation hut," Frank said. "Don't rightly know how much longer she'll be."

"That's okay. I didn't really plan to stop. It just kind of..." Her words trailed off. She turned to Parker. "You ready?"

"Anytime."

Suddenly Cindy couldn't get into the car fast enough. "Give Sheri my best, okay, Frank?"

"Will do."

"So," Cindy said as they reached the highway. "You wanted to know about me. Now you know."

"And now?" Parker said.

"Now I want you to show me where *you* grew up."

The neighborhood Parker drove her through had the subtle air of affluence she expected. Shadowy shapes denoted mature landscaping and fancy fences that didn't interfere with the residents' view. Motion sensor lights blinked on as Parker drove down the dark driveway and killed the Mustang's engine. He turned to Cindy.

"You want to get out? Look around?"

"Soitinly," she said with a fake accent that shrilled through the silent night air.

Before she stepped from the car she reached down and slipped off her shoes and stockings. The carefully cultivated lawn felt like a thick carpet underfoot, damp and cool on her feet as she followed her guide. A trellised archway smothered with fragrant roses, their pale petals agleam like freshly churned cream, showed the way to the back of the house.

Parker stood, hands in his pockets, looking up the trunk of an old tree. "My tree house is still up there." He pointed. "Stole my first kiss there."

Cindy ripped her gaze from the sprawling bungalow, its walls twined in bougainvillea, to the shadowy outline of the tree house. "Let's go up!" She put her foot on the first rung nailed to the tree's sturdy trunk and felt it come off under her weight. "Rats."

"Hasn't been used in a while, I'd guess."

Unsettled emotions propelled her to where the pool beckoned, its smooth surface shimmering from the glow of the underwater lights, and she turned to Parker. "Last one in is a rotten egg."

"You're not serious?"

"You don't feel like a midnight skinny dip? Well I do." Putting her words to action she skinned out of her dress and panties, trusting the darkness to veil her as she dove into the pool. The warm, silken water enwrapped her weightlessly. She surfaced, tossed back her hair and laughed up at him.

"I dare you."

"Cindy."

"Double-dare."

She could see the gleam of his smile in the shadow of his face as he started to unbutton his shirt. "That does it. Never could resist a double-dare."

Cindy dove down and swam underwater to the far side of the pool while Parker stripped. As she reached the end she surfaced and followed the sound of a loud splash. Where was he? She felt something whisk by her foot as she held onto the pool's edge. A scant second later he bobbed into sight an arm's length away. "Race you to the other end."

"Go!" Cindy yelled, giving herself a mighty push with her feet and what she hoped was a head start. Head start or not, he caught up to her easily and kept pace alongside her so they both reached the far end at the same time. Breathlessly Cindy shook her wet hair out of her eyes.

"Where's your sense of competition, Davis? You had me."

"Do I have you?" Parker edged disturbingly close. Before she could inch back he reached out and clasped her face between his hands. "Winner gets a kiss," he said in a husky tone.

"It was a tie," Cindy said, unable to still the shiver that rippled through her at the feel of his strong fingers cupping her face.

"Then we both win."

Cindy grabbed the edge of the pool for support as his lips closed over hers lightly, teasingly, playfully. Except there was nothing playful in her body's response. It was immediate, a heavy rush of heat that saturated her limbs. If Parker didn't have hold of her she would have surely sunk like a rock.

As his mouth shaped itself to hers, her lips opened automatically, anticipating the liquid exploration of his tongue. She clasped his shoulder with her free hand, as much to support herself as to keep distance between them, half afraid that if Parker's muscular chest brushed her breasts she just might come apart in his arms.

Abruptly the patio light blinked on. A woman's voice called out. "Parker?"

"Busted," Parker murmured against her lips.

"Parker, is that you?"

The kiss ended on a regretful sigh from him. "Yes, Mother."

"Are you alone?"

He slanted a grin at Cindy. "No, Mother."

"Is that lovely girl from the wedding with you?"

"Yes, Mother."

"Bring her in after you dry off. I could regale her with a few old stories of other times I caught you in here with a girl at night."

"It was all her idea."

"That was always your line of defense. Can't you come up with a new one?"

"Mother!"

"I'm joking. Good night, Parker. Good night, Cindy."

"Good night, Mrs. Davis."

The door closed, the light clicked off, leaving them once more alone. Cindy swam toward the ladder.

"Don't get out yet," Parker said.

"Why not?"

"I know my mother. She'll be back in a minute with robes and towels."

He watched Cindy float and deliberately kept his distance. He'd sensed a streak of recklessness running through her, growing as the night wore on. It made her as unpredictable as the wild animals up in Tom's compound. You never knew if you'd get bitten or kissed. Or both.

His mother appeared with fluffy towels and robes she'd warmed in the dryer and they dried and dressed in silence. The difference in their two backgrounds could hardly have been more pronounced.

"I made coffee," Robin called out the window once they were decent. "And the peach cobbler's fresh-made today from my own peaches.

"Do you mind?" Parker asked, low-voiced. "She gets lonely at night when Dad's out at the hospital."

"No, I don't mind."

Inside the homey kitchen, Parker pulled out a stool at the kitchen bar and helped Cindy get settled.

"Did we miss anything important after the wedding supper?" Cindy asked.

"Only Bambi's father making a spectacle of himself. Mercifully Gord got paged and we could make our escape."

"Lifesavers, those pagers," Parker drawled.

"What a lovely surprise," Robin said brightly, scooping mounds of ice cream into the bowls of peach cobbler. "The coffee's decaf. I hope that's okay. Gord says it's better for me at night."

"Since when do you listen to what Dad says is best for you?" Parker teased.

"For your information, your father and I have had to practice a fair bit of give-and-take over the years," Robin said. "Your father's not always right, despite what he thinks."

Parker sobered. "Yeah, but I never heard so much as a disagreement between you two when I was growing up."

"That doesn't mean we didn't have differences of opinion."

"I beg you. Don't suddenly shatter my illusions now."

Robin glanced over at Cindy in mock frustration. "Don't ask me how I raised such an idealist."

"Come on, Mom. Things *were* pretty much ideal."

"Hardly by a long shot. Your father and I started life as a married couple without the blessing of your grandparents."

"Nana and Pops? They think Dad is the greatest."

"Now they do. They've conveniently forgotten their initial opposition to the union."

"But why?"

"Social standing and economics. Your father was a penniless orphan working two jobs when we met. Dreaming about medical school. They were convinced he was after the family money, so made it very clear there'd be no help coming from that quarter. We were young and in love and learned the hard way love doesn't pay the rent or put food on the table.

"They shook their head disapprovingly as I worked and put Gord through med school. Predicted that once he had that M.D. after his name I'd be left high and dry. They were very convincing in their convictions."

Parker shook his head in disbelief. "How come you never told me this story before?"

"I didn't want you to think any less of your grandparents, I suppose. And it's pretty much forgotten on their side. They think the sun rises and sets on Gordon. Once he was able to support me in a fitting manner."

"And here I thought things were always effortless for the two of you."

"Nothing is ever effortless. I moved from a house with daily household help to a pretty much flea-infested dump that was more than we could afford. Don't think I wasn't tempted once or twice to chuck it all. To run home like the little princess I'd been raised to think I was. I'm sure there were times your father wished I would. And many's the time he felt inadequate over his lack of ability to shower me with nice things."

"How'd it all change?"

"Your father started his practice. You were born. Nana and Pops tried to buy us a house. Gord flat-out refused to accept their help. No one ever refused

Pops. It kind of turned around his thinking toward your father.''

''You telling old tales?'' Gord entered the kitchen and nibbled on Robin's shoulder. Parker was used to open signs of affection between his parents, but Cindy shifted on her stool as if uncomfortable.

''I'm explaining to Cindy why Parker is unreasonably idealistic. Apparently we did him a disservice by keeping our disagreements to ourselves.''

Gord winked broadly in Parker's direction. ''The secret of marital harmony. I always let your mother have her own way. Period.''

''That's why you won't slow down long enough to take me on that cruise I've always wanted to go on.''

''I will. I told you. One day.''

Robin rolled her eyes. ''Silly me. I want to go before someone's pushing me around in a wheelchair and I'm wearing a diaper.''

It was clearly an old argument. ''I'm tired, Rob. We'll talk about this later.''

''See, Parker? Not in front of the children. Gord, he's old enough to know married life is not perfect.''

''Sure,'' Gord said, pressing a kiss to her brow. ''But let him continue to think his old man is perfect.''

''The stories I could tell,'' Robin said. But she stood and folded herself into her husband's arms in a gesture of support and trust and love that struck Parker as more intimate than any long, wet, hungry kiss the two of them might share. Parker took the opportunity for him and Cindy to say their good-nights.

Once settled in the Mustang and headed for the highway, Cindy turned to Parker. "You're lucky. You scored a real mother."

"What's a real mother?"

"One who bakes pies and goes to PTA meetings."

"Your mother didn't bake?"

"My mother was fifteen when I was born. Don't get me wrong, I have scads of respect for her. It can't have been easy being a mother when you're still a kid yourself. And she took real good care of me."

Cindy lapsed into silence as she burrowed into the thick hand-knit sweater Mrs. Davis had insisted she borrow. Such a gesture would never have occurred to her own mother, but Parker's mother's thoughtfulness made Cindy feel all snuggly and fuzzy inside.

She pivoted in her seat to face Parker as he navigated the car along the coast road. "I should really go home. It's getting late."

"Past midnight," Parker agreed. "The dress is still in one piece. Both shoes still with us? Yup, even if they're not on your feet. Besides, here we are at my place." As he spoke, the car purred to a stop. Cindy looked around but couldn't see a thing in the pitch black.

"Where do you live? The side of a mountain?"

"Better. Come on." He pulled a flashlight out of the back seat and helped her from the car. The feeble light wasn't much of a deterrent against the darkness.

All Cindy could see were shadowy dark bushes lining an equally shadowy pathway. She hadn't gone more than three hesitant steps before Parker swooped her up in his arms.

"What are you doing? Put me down."

"Settle down. I know my way blindfolded. Besides, I've never carried a woman over the threshold before."

"Why me? Why now?"

"Because you're barefoot. And light enough that I can carry you without injuring myself, thus feeling extremely macho in the process."

"Very gallant," Cindy murmured. But she looped her arms around Parker's neck and laid her head drowsily against his shoulder.

She could hear the sound of the ocean waves close by, smell that rich, briny air.

"Don't tell me you live in a cottage on the water, rich boy?"

"Better. I live in a cottage that hangs right out over the water."

Parker made his way across what appeared to be some sort of drawbridge and put Cindy down while he unlocked the door.

"Come on." He reached inside and turned on a light, which glowed softly out of the windows and revealed their destination to be a converted boathouse.

Cindy followed him inside, looking around her in awe. "I know this place. I've kayaked past. It has those huge garage doors so you can open up the entire front of the house."

"I installed them myself."

The boathouse's interior was one huge space, divided into kitchen and living quarters. Weathered wood floors were visible beneath colored rugs used to divide the space. A telescope was set up on one side and faced due west. Cindy glanced from the sleek, low-slung couches up to the open beams dotted with plants, rugs and sculpture. A curved metal staircase led to the loft and what she guessed to be Parker's bedroom.

"How long have you lived here?"

"About five years," Parker said. "It belonged to my aunt and uncle. After my uncle died and my aunt sold his boat she didn't know what to do with it. I made some inquiries and found out that as long as it was attached to the land and had its own waste disposal system, I could do the conversion."

"Not many people can boast about actually fishing from their front deck." Cindy spoke with more than a tinge of envy. She plopped herself on the stool and peered through the telescope. "Oh, my."

"Isn't it great?" Parker came up behind her and laid a companionable hand on her shoulder.

"I wish I'd known you when the comet was hanging around. You would have never got rid of me."

"Who says I'd have wanted to?"

"Oh." Cindy slithered gracelessly off the stool and

away from Parker's hold. "I've been known to make a right royal nuisance of myself."

She turned, hands clasped behind her back in an unconscious little-girl pose. "So. Wasn't this something? You've seen where I live and where I grew up. I've seen where you live and where you grew up."

"Don't go all skittish on me, Cinderella."

"What makes you say that?"

"I know skittish when I see it. Come see upstairs."

Cindy hung back.

"There's a big huge skylight over the bed. It's like being on top of a mountain."

"I think I've seen enough for one night, thanks." Cindy faked a yawn. "It really is awfully late."

Parker subjected her to a long, level glance. "You're right. It is getting late." As he doused the lights Cindy felt herself cloaked in the wonderful magic darkness that is only possible on a special night with a special companion. She didn't really want to leave. So why was she? One word from her and—

But the word had to come from her.

Fear gripped her insides.

Fear that she'd say the wrong thing.

Was saying the wrong thing worse than saying nothing?

He stood near the door, waiting. Cindy cast one last glance around the room. Moonlight glinted on a crystal hanging in the window near the table. The effect was hypnotic. She couldn't tear her gaze away.

She wasn't aware of Parker having moved, but suddenly he was at her side. He laid a hand on her arm.

"You sure you want to go?"

"No. Yes. I don't know."

She gazed imploringly up at him. Somewhere, probably downtown, she heard the muffled sound of a clock chime the hour. It was 2:00 a.m.

He tilted her chin up and kissed her softly. Reassuringly. "I want you to be sure."

# *Chapter Eight*

Cindy reached up and grazed the outline of his jaw with her fingertips. "Is anyone ever really sure?" She felt his jaw clench.

"Don't look to me for assurances, Cinderella. I'm fresh out."

Cindy moistened her lips with her tongue. From her earliest recollections she had always known exactly what she wanted and grabbed for it hard and fast. So why the hesitation? Tonight, at this moment, she wanted Parker. Everything else ceased to matter.

"And if I don't need assurances?" she said softly.

"What do you need?"

She heard the uncertainty in his voice and realized that he wasn't all that sure of himself or her answer. She looked up, saw her image reflected in his eyes and swallowed thickly.

She was not drowning.

Not losing herself in him.

She was in full control of the situation. "I need you."

He exhaled heavily, as if he'd been holding his breath. "I'm awful glad to hear you say that." As he gathered her against him hip to hip, breastbone to breastbone, she could feel the heavy thud of his heart against her breast. Her every nerve ending tingled in response, as if a million megawatts of electricity had been transmitted through him to her.

Arms snugged around each others' waists they climbed the staircase to the bedroom.

Parker hadn't exaggerated. The skylight encompassed almost the entire ceiling, exposing a star-studded canopy of sky. An open window provided a symphony of sounds as the waves lapped at the pilings beneath the house.

"If I lived here, I'd never leave," Cindy said. "Never."

Parker busied himself with the zipper on her dress. "Till now it's been somewhat on the lonely side."

Cindy attacked the buttons on his shirt, measured, precise movements effectively masking her inner lack of assurance. "Just so you know. The first time with someone, well I don't expect much."

Parker raised a brow. "Gee, thanks."

"I mean it's always awkward and stuff. Much better to get it over with."

"Get it over with," Parker echoed.

"You know. Behind us. And then if we want to get together again sometime, well, there's no first-time awkwardness. It'll be much better."

Parker caught her hands in both of his and stilled

her movements. "A word of warning. I don't do one-night stands, Cinderella. Never have."

"You say that now. But who knows how you'll feel afterward? I mean, if it turns out to be a mistake it's best to admit that right away and move on, don't you think? Rather than belabor the point."

Parker crossed his arms over a tautly muscled chest that was the result of hard manual labor, not free weights in a gym. "I have to hand it to you. You sure know how to ruin a good seduction."

"I just think it's best to be up front about these things. Realistic and all."

"You've got a real gift for pushing folks away, anytime you feel them start to get too close, you know that?"

"Guilty as charged." Cindy punctuated her words with an awkward laugh. "Marissa says it's my safety valve. To not let someone near me until I'm convinced they need me more than I need them."

"And if I tell you I need you? Naked and in my bed."

"That's precisely what I needed to hear." She shrugged and her dress pooled at her feet like a puddle of spilled red wine. Reverently Parker reached to touch her breasts, grazing them lightly with the palms of his hands. Cindy swallowed a gasp at her body's instant response. A lightning bolt of heat chased her length and set her aflame.

"The way you make me feel," she murmured, as her lips found his. Together they swayed from side to side, locked in the special dance of lovers. Hands, tongues, lips and lashes, touched, teased, tasted.

Parker eased her gently to the bed and skimmed off her panties. Her legs parted and she felt him explore her damp heat. He stepped back and, despite her murmured protest, stood gazing down at her splayed and wanton across the bright Aztec-design bedspread.

"You're beautiful in the moonlight," he said huskily as he undid his belt and stepped out of his pants.

"So are you." Cindy gave a sensuous stretch, hands overhead. Above her, Parker was symmetry in motion, all hard angles and planes, well-defined muscles peppered with dark hair. He stretched atop her and rolled so they lay on their sides, joined at all the crucial junctions. Cindy felt impatience sear through her and forced herself to slow down. To meet and match his leisurely hand-and-mouth discovery of her curves, creases and hidden crevices.

He feasted on her. And she upon him, marveling anew at the study in contrasts. Sinewy, ropy muscle. The softest underflesh. Despite hair-roughed legs and callused hands the skin on his back felt as soft and smooth as any newborn's.

She tunneled her fingers through the springy thickness of his hair as he suckled at her breasts, his actions sending a fresh wave of need to the core of her womanhood.

"Parker," she murmured.

"Mmm?"

"We didn't talk about protection."

"I've got it covered."

"I thought you would, but I needed to make sure."

"I'd expect no less of you."

As she felt him dampen himself with her dewy love juices and ready the way for his entry, she took a deep breath and reminded herself to relax. Told herself Parker needed her far more than she needed him.

At the moment of penetration, undulating waves of pleasure wiped away any and all thought of need or want. Every feeling she had centered solely on the magic of the moment and the man who made it all possible.

CINDY AWOKE TO the fragrant smell of fresh-baked bread and just-brewed coffee. She bolted upright in bed and turned to Parker, who slept alongside her. How was that possible? Surely he didn't have his own personal Mary Poppins who showed up with piping hot rolls every morning.

"Parker." She poked his shoulder. "Parker."

He woke, rolled and draped himself across her mid-section.

"Parker. Who's downstairs cooking?"

"What?" He sat up and rubbed his eyes with the heels of his hand.

"Someone is cooking downstairs. I can smell it."

Parker laughed and launched himself at her, sending her flying back against the pillows.

"Bread machine's on a timer. So's the coffee."

Cindy used both hand to push him off of her. "You're kidding. You wake up to this every day?"

He rolled to his back and pillowed his arms beneath his head, wishbone style. "Give it a try. You'll see it's not such a bad way to live."

Cindy slid hastily from the bed and reached for her clothes.

"What's the matter? Where are you going?"

"It's too much."

"What do you mean, 'too much'? What's too much?"

She wriggled into her dress. "Everything. You. This place. The way you live. I have to think about this."

"Who's stopping you?"

"I mean, I have to think long and hard about this, someplace you aren't."

Parker sighed and pushed aside the covers. "I'll drive you home."

Cindy looked away quickly before her resolve deserted her. She couldn't allow herself to weaken. Not now. She raked her fingers through her hair. Thank goodness it always looked uncombed. "I'd rather walk. I need to clear my head."

Parker flopped back against the pillows. "Have it your way. But I've got to tell you. You're missing out on a great breakfast."

"Bye, Parker." She laid his mother's sweater across the end of the bed. "Thank your mom for me for the use of her sweater, okay?"

Seconds later as he heard the door slam behind her,

he stared up out the skylight as if the heavens might hold the answers he sought. Then he catapulted out of bed. Since the heavens didn't provide any immediate answers, he knew someone who might.

CINDY'S MOM looked more like Cindy's sister than her parent. Same graceful limbs, beautiful big hands and feet. Right now those long, supple fingers were caked in clay as Sheri worked her potter's wheel. Her blond hair was a shade or two lighter than Cindy's, streaked with white-gold that on another woman would be called gray. But her smooth yet sexy voice was the same as her daughter's. Along with her thoughtful frown.

"Cindy always was an independent thing. I used to figure it was on account of what happened when she was born."

"What happened when she was born?"

"You say she told you about me?" Sheri slanted him a laser-sharp glance.

"Even brought me out here to show me where she grew up."

"She's never done that before. You must be someone special in her life."

"I'd like to be. Trouble is, she keeps pushing me away."

"That makes two of us." She studied him more closely. "She brought you out here but never came to find me. What's that tell you?"

"Frank told us you were in the meditation shed."

Sheri almost laughed. "There's irony. I was meditating, asking the universe for my daughter back and she was here, not wanting to disturb me. That effectively sums up our relationship right there. What all did she tell you?''

"She told me you were a teenage mom. And despite your youth, you never made her feel unwanted or unloved.''

"That's good to know, I guess.'' The clay on the wheel mushed down into a misshapen pancake and Sheri let out an exasperated sound. She plunged her hands and arms into a bucket of water at her feet and took her time to wipe off the clay with a nearly threadbare towel. Then she swiveled around on her stool to face Parker.

"I was fifteen. Everyone told me to put her up for adoption. And for a while I thought they might be right, but I couldn't make up my mind and I refused to sign any papers.''

"So you kept her.''

"My parents wouldn't let me take her home. Back then there were no foster homes in Madronna Beach, as you can imagine.''

"So what happened?''

"Cindy stayed in the hospital nursery till I got set up here and could go get her.''

"How long was she in the hospital?''

"Nearly a month,'' Sheri said. "So we never got that initial bonding time that's supposedly so important. And I truly believe, in my heart of hearts, that's the reason Cindy won't let anyone close. She was never huggy as a baby, never wanted to cuddle. My little girl started life off on her own and decided this is the way it's supposed to be. And for Cindy, that's the way she's made it.''

"You READY?'' Cindy blew into Marissa's place impatiently.

"I've changed my mind. You go ahead without me.'' Marissa almost seemed to cower. What was up with that? Marissa *never* backed down from a challenge. *Never!*

Cindy squatted next to her friend. "Come on, Rissa. Don't be a party-pooper. I borrowed Jan's van and everything.'' They had been planning this trip for several days. On Cindy's day off they would head up to Tom's compound. After all, Cindy reasoned, just because her own personal life was a shambles didn't mean she couldn't play cupid for her friend. She'd never seen Marissa so taken with a man as she seemed to be with Tom. He was practically all she could talk about.

"And I appreciate all the trouble you've gone to, really I do. But I'm not ready.''

Cindy stood. "It's because he's never seen you in your chair, isn't it?''

Marissa shrugged. "People treat me different, Cin. You've seen them. They talk to me like I'm a small child. Tom just looked at me…'' She sighed.

"So you give the man another chance to look at you.''

"Maybe I'm happier just holding on to the memory.''

"It's not like you to back down from taking a risk."

"Is that so?" Marissa said. "Guess I've been hanging around you too much."

"What's that supposed to mean?"

"I know you blew Parker off. Started to get close and ran scared."

"Smart ass," Cindy said. "Come on, let's go."

"Does he know we're coming?"

"Nope," Cindy said cheerfully. "And I'm willing to bet he's a guy who gets very few surprises in his life."

Cindy drove Jan's catering van slowly up the gravel trail to Tom's compound, trying not to jounce Marissa around too much. Her friend was quiet on the trip, hands clasped tightly in her lap, her lips thin, eyes straight ahead.

Relationships, Cindy thought. Sure did make a stir-fry out of people's lives.

"Morning, Tom," she said breezily, pulling up and screeching to a dusty stop alongside of him before she hopped from the van. "I brought along a helper."

"That a fact? You're getting to be a regular fixture up here."

"You wish!" Cindy scoffed. But she hesitated. Was he trying to tell her not to come so often?

His next words alleviated her fears. "You don't see me complaining about an extra set of hands, do you?"

"That's what I thought. I believe you've already met my best friend, Marissa." She didn't miss the way Tom froze as she opened the passenger door.

Marissa dimpled prettily. "I hope you don't mind my barging in uninvited. Cindy said it would be okay. I won't be in the way. Honest."

The look on Tom's face was absolutely priceless. He stepped up to the van, removed his dusty Stetson, took one of Marissa's hands in his, and cleared his throat a couple of times.

"I'm honored. Please visit us as often as you would like."

"Us?" Marissa looked confused.

Tom waved his hat toward the cages. "My boarders."

"Ah." Cindy caught Marissa's palpable air of relief. It must be contagious. She was impressed with the way Tom acted toward her friend.

"So what's to do, Tom?" Cindy asked, once she had Marissa's chair set up next to the van.

Tom didn't seem to hear her. He was still staring at Marissa as if afraid she might vanish from his sight.

"Tom?"

"Oh," he said. "Whatever you feel like. I'm going to give your friend the grand tour. May I?"

Without further ado he lifted Marissa from the van and stood with her in his arms. Marissa looped her arms around his neck, leaned her head on his shoulder and gave a gentle sigh. Cindy doubted either of them even remembered she was there.

# Chapter Nine

"How'd it go?" Jan asked as Cindy passed her the keys to the van. "Is Cupid's job done?"

"And then some, I'd say. I left them up there. Tom'll bring her home, whenever."

"If ever?" Jan suggested.

"She can't stay up there, even if she wants to. It's hardly wheelchair friendly."

"But you're feeling displaced, nonetheless," Jan said shrewdly. "Marissa was always there when you needed her."

"You've got it all wrong, Jan. I don't need Marissa. She needs me. Or at least she did."

"Whatever you say, doll."

Cindy was thinking about what Jan said as she walked home. Was there any truth to her friend's words? Like maybe even a glimmer? She was kind of used to Marissa's background presence and getting together had been always her call, on her terms. Marissa kept herself busy when Cindy wasn't around, always made time for her and never made her feel badly about time lapsing between her visits.

She heard a truck drive up behind her and slow to a crawl. She flicked a quick glance over her shoulder. Sure enough, Parker Davis. It was a small town. He'd doubtless driven past her countless times over the years, but today felt compelled to stop and chat. Why was that?

"You busy?" he called out.

Cindy resisted the urge to roll her eyes. How busy did she look?

Knowing it would be rude to keep walking, she made her way over to his vehicle. He leaned across and opened the door. "Hop in."

"Just cruising around, in between bus runs, offering rides to those who'd rather walk?" she asked with what she considered to be just the right amount of sarcasm. Caustic, but not cutting.

"I'm heading to an estate sale up in Deep Bay." He paused as if the idea had just struck. "You should come."

"I don't think so."

"I understand they had quite the library," he said coaxingly.

Parker was very clearly a man used to getting his own way, something she'd known from their first meeting. "What are you going there for?"

"They also had quite the wine cellar. It's my folks' anniversary coming up. I thought it would be a kick to pick them up something special."

In spite of herself, Cindy was impressed. "That's a very thoughtful gift."

"I'm just that kind of guy," he said. "You with me?"

"Sure. Why not?" she said as she climbed up into the cab of the truck. Truth be told, she was excited at the prospect of estate sale books. It had been ages since she'd splurged on anything that wasn't an absolute necessity.

As was their custom, they passed the drive in an easy, comfortable silence. Cindy liked that Parker wasn't a chatterbox. Eventually it was she who broke the quiet.

"I've never been to Deep Bay. What's it like?"

"About the same size as Madronna, but different energy. It used to be quite the fishing community. Less artsy and affluent, more working class. It reminds me of parts of Portugal."

"You've been to Europe?" She tried to keep the envy out of her voice. Of course he'd been to Europe. His upbringing no doubt afforded him unlimited travel opportunities.

"It was a long time ago. Right out of high school."

Trying to forget about Tammy, Cindy surmised as she scrunched against the door, ignoring the way the door handle dug into her hip. She caught herself and straightened. Why was she trying to physically distance herself from Parker? What she *ought* to be doing was *emotionally* distancing herself. For she'd thought about him way too often since they'd made love. And even now, with half a bench seat between them, she was aware of his strength and presence, his scent, his body heat. It was like a magnetic signal, reaching out and touching her. One she was powerless to ignore.

"This looks like the place." Parker signaled and turned between two huge stone pillars, down a long driveway lined with bougainvillea.

"What a gorgeous spot," Cindy said. She half turned to face Parker as he pulled the truck to a stop behind a dozen or so other vehicles in the circular driveway. "How did you hear about this sale, anyway?"

"Buddy of mine owns an antique shop. He's in the loop and knew I was looking for something special for the folks."

"I'm glad I ran into you today," Cindy said, and recognized the truth in her words. She usually spent whatever free time she had with Marissa. Now it looked as if Tom might have usurped that privilege.

Parker shot her his "look," one she was coming to know quite well.

"What?" In spite of herself, she was unable to keep the defensive edge from her tone.

He smiled ruefully. "This was no accidental run-in, Cindy. I'd been to your place already and left a note on the door. Then I bumped into Jan, who told me that you'd borrowed her van but promised to have it back by noon because she needed it."

"What you're saying, then, is this was no coincidence, you coming along just when you did." She didn't know if she ought to be flattered or annoyed.

"Not in the slightest. I was determined to find you and convince you to come out with me."

"Madronna might be small enough for you to track me down, but there were no guarantees I'd join you."

Parker shrugged easily. "I figured I'd take my chances. Fifty-fifty odds and all."

"Fifty-fifty?" Cindy said, not without some amusement. "How'd you figure?"

"Seems to be my success rate where you're concerned."

She burst out laughing in spite of herself. "You are something else, Parker Davis."

"Thanks. Shall we?"

"Let's."

The house was circa 1920s, its contents under the watchful eye of several security guards, one of whom indicated the way to the library.

"Oh, my word!" Cindy stopped point-blank in the doorway and breathed in the ambrosial smell of old leather-bound books. Some were shelved, while others were boxed in small lots, separated by subject and author.

Parker gave her elbow a quick squeeze. "Enjoy. I'll be back after I visit the wine cellar. Unless you want to come along."

Cindy gave her head a quick shake. "I'm sure the wine cellar is equally fascinating, but since my wine knowledge is limited to current vintages, I'll stay put here, thanks."

Many of the books were rare first editions, far beyond her means but still a delight to see and to handle. A row of white cotton gloves was on the table near the doorway and she slid a pair onto her hands before carefully and reverently delving into boxes and shelves. She had no idea how much time had passed or who came and went from the room; she was in her own little world, tucked into a leather wing chair, lost in the first edition of Clement C. Moore's *'Twas the Night Before Christmas.*

"Something catch your fancy?" Parker hunkered down alongside her chair.

With a weighty sigh she closed the cover and passed the book to him. "Check out the illustrations."

"Wow," he said. "You going to take it?"

She shook her head. "Ironic, isn't it? I collect old Christmas books, because as a kid there was never a Santa Claus. Yet I gravitate to the whole fantasy."

"We all need childhood dreams," Parker said. "Even as adults. Sure you're not going to take the book?"

"I don't even dare ask how much. I feel happy just to have held it for a short while."

Parker nodded and stood, still clasping the book in one hand. "Did you see this?"

"What?"

"Books on animal husbandry, circa nineteenth century. Reasonable, too."

"You have a talent," Cindy said. "How was the wine cellar? Find what you came for?"

"This ought to do the trick." He presented a dusty bottle of Château Latour, 1970, with a flourish.

Cindy pretended she could decipher the label. "Very nice. Will they drink it or save it?"

Parker laughed. "Trust me. It's a first-growth and ready to drink now. They'll enjoy it on their anniversary, for sure. One thing my parents taught me is to seize the moment, because you never know what the Fates might have in store for you later on."

"Is that on account of your father being a doctor?"

"Part of it, I imagine. But I think it also tends to be simple life philosophy."

"Too bad more people don't live that way," Cindy said. "Instead of waiting till the time is right, or they have the mortgage paid off, or the kids are grown."

"Exactly," Parker said. "Opportunity missed."

In the end, Cindy left, dusty but happy with her collection of animal husbandry books and several hand-written pioneer journals by early settlers that she considered had been grossly underpriced, much too tempting to pass up.

Parker totally blew her mind by purchasing the Moore book. "I didn't know you were a fan of Moore and Christmas stories."

"There's a lot you don't know about me. Maybe one day I'll get to read this to my kids. And teach them to revere first editions." He wrapped the bottle of wine carefully in a wad of bubble-wrap and placed her box of books on the seat between them, seat-belted in. "Everybody safe and ready to go?"

"That was thoroughly enjoyable," Cindy said as they headed back to Madronna Beach. "Thank you for thinking of me."

Parker cocked her another one of his "looks." "I

always think about you these days. I'm just not quite sure what to do about it.''

''Oh.'' Cindy scrunched down a little in her seat. She thought about him, too, but it was nothing she cared to admit so brazenly.

''But that's my problem.'' He gave her hand a light squeeze. ''And being able to share today with you. That's my pleasure.''

They drove in silence for several miles until abruptly Parker swore and braked to a sudden stop. Cindy grabbed for the books and wine like a mother might secure an infant.

''What's wrong? What is it?''

But he'd already leapt from the truck without a word and started running back down the road. That's when Cindy saw what he had seen. A recent skid mark veered off of the road and over the bank. She started to run as well. Parker paused to chuck his cell phone at her.

''Stay here,'' he said. ''You might need to call for help.'' After which he skidded and bounded through the broken scrub underbrush to a car, halfway down the hillside, which luckily appeared to be right side up.

Cindy watched, her heart in her throat, as Parker opened the driver's door and stuck his head inside the vehicle. Staying put had never been easy for her and this time was no exception. She picked her way cautiously down the bank in time to see Parker help a dazed but seemingly otherwise unharmed young man from the car.

"Is he all right?"

Parker flashed her an impatient look. "Stay with him. His girlfriend's still inside." He rounded the car to the passenger door while Cindy tended to the young driver.

"What's your name?"

"Mike Mitchell."

"What day is it, Mike?"

"It's Sunday."

"Do you know where you are?"

"In the bushes." He flashed her a rueful smile. "Took that last turn a little too fast." He looked over at the car. "Is Sandy okay? I heard her scream as we went over the bank."

Cindy glanced over to where Parker was leading a young girl toward them. "She looks okay. We'll know in a minute."

Parker fetched the first aid kit from his truck and applied salve and Band-Aids to the young couple's bruises and scrapes.

"You'll be sore for a few days," he said. "Do you have any idea just how lucky you both are?"

Mike hung his head. "It's my fault. I lost control on the gravel shoulder and spun over the edge."

"Speeding, from the looks of your skid marks."

"Are you going to call the police?" Mike mumbled.

"I ought to," Parker said. "You could have killed yourselves. To say nothing of someone else."

"I'll lose my license," Mike said. "Then I won't

be able to get to work. We're saving up to get married.''

"Little late to be thinking about that, isn't it?" Parker said sternly. "The speeding limits are there for a reason, you know."

Mike nodded shakily and put his arm around his girlfriend. Parker appeared to consider the two of them.

How young they both looked, Cindy thought. Young and scared. Far too young to be considering marriage. And far too young to have their lives end out here on this desolate stretch of highway. She wondered what Parker would do.

"Tell you what," Parker said finally. "Where do you live?"

"Deep Bay." They both spoke at once.

"I'll tow you out. And won't report you on one condition."

"Anything," Mike said with freckle-faced earnestness.

"You enroll in a defensive driving course. Learn some road safety skills."

"I can do that."

"I bet you can," Parker said. "Because I'm going to check and make sure that you do."

Cindy and Sandy stood well back out of the way as Parker moved his truck into position, applied the tow line to Mike's car and winched it back up to the road. Cindy listened to the young girl's nervous chatter and let her babble on about Mike and their marriage plans.

The car, like its occupants, had suffered only a few minor dents and scratches. The young couple waved gratefully as they turned around and drove slowly back in the direction of Deep Bay.

"That was a really decent thing you did, helping them out and giving them that break."

Parker frowned. "I only hope to God I did the right thing."

"He seemed scared enough that the lesson will stick," Cindy said. "I'm sure they appreciate what you did." She turned. "Will you really check and make sure he takes that driving education class?"

"Count on it," Parker said.

Cindy smiled. "You are a good big brother. The crusading white knight, aren't you? It's kind of a natural role for you."

"The superhero's cape's a little tattered these days," Parker said. "But I do like to help out when I can. Hopefully Mike won't make the same mistake again. Having the kid sit around out of work sure won't solve a thing."

"Well," Cindy said, "you've certainly done your good deed for the day."

They stood there alongside the truck, sexual chemistry just sizzling between them, and Cindy thought for sure he was going to kiss her. She actually took a half step closer, and couldn't quite credit the flood of disappointment when he turned and opened the door of the truck for her.

"We should get going."

"Right," Cindy said, climbing up into the cab. "It's getting late and I've got lots to do."

She cast a possessive look at her box of books between them on the seat, then up at Parker. "Thanks for everything today."

He shrugged as they resumed their journey. "I didn't do anything special."

Cindy realized that he meant what he said. Being thoughtful, considerate of others, helping where he could, were all ingrained character traits, things Parker did as naturally as other people breathe.

THE FOLLOWING DAY found Cindy at the beach. It was early enough that the place was still deserted. Cindy reached the sand and kicked off her sandals, pulling in a deep lungful of air. Farther out she could see a huge bank of fog, blanketing the water and obscuring the horizon. In a short time the summer solstice sun would have burned off the fog, giving the illusion one could see forever.

Cindy buried her nose in the single red rose she carried and stepped into the icy Pacific. By the time she reached mid-calf her toes were numb from the cold, her legs tingling.

*Be careful what she wished for!*

She'd started her own summer solstice ritual the summer she turned fifteen and never missed a year. She kept her wishes simple. Inner peace. A sense of belonging. A good sense of self. Abstract wishes that she could rationalize came true.

This year she paused, not wanting to be too greedy.

Win the race? Enough money for her tuition? Fall in love?

She started. Where did that thought pop up from, with Parker's face attached? Love meant dependency. Didn't it? She took a breath and tossed the rose as far as she could. It crested the waves and bobbed out to sea, a tiny red dot of crimson. Then she waded to shore, picked up her sandals and let the sun warm her cold feet while she stared at the tiny red dot that symbolized her wish till it vanished from sight. Then she headed for the shoe store.

Parker stood in the doorway to the Glass Slipper and admired those great gams as Cindy clambered up and down the ladder, fetching and carrying an armload of shoe boxes to a heavy woman with badly swollen ankles. One at a time Cindy slid dozens of shoes onto the woman's stubby foot, alternately nodding or shaking her head, until the miracle happened. They discovered the perfect shoe. The woman's face lit up as if Cindy had presented her with a fabulous gift and Parker bit back a smile as he watched the sale's satisfactory conclusion. What a girl, his Cinderella.

He stopped himself with a frown. *His* Cinderella?

Sure, he liked Cindy a lot. But if he started getting all possessive toward her, heaven knew she'd bolt faster than a wild horse that smells the glue wagon's approach.

He stepped aside as the happy customer left, squared his shoulders, tucked his hands into his jeans pockets and pasted a friendly, nonthreatening smile on his face as he entered the shop.

"Hi there."

"Hi there, yourself." But he caught the way she lowered her eyes to the cash desk and refused to meet his gaze.

"I've been thinking about you."

She looked up then, clear green eyes troubled. "Me, too."

"So, how come you didn't return my calls?"

"That's why."

"Because you were thinking about me?"

"Right, first time out of the gate." Cindy made her way from behind the desk and across the store, where she started to ball up scattered socks and stockings. After which she busied herself stuffing the rejected footwear back into tissue-paper cocoons.

Parker stilled her movement with a hand on her arm. Gently tugged her up and around to face him.

"I told you before. I don't do one-night stands."

"And I told you before. I need some time to think."

"Why do you think I stayed away as long as I could stand it? Didn't we have a good time the other day at the estate sale?"

"We did." She glanced pointedly to where his fingers ringed her forearm. "Which doesn't give you leave to come in here and strong-arm me at your whim. I told you I'd call when I was ready."

"I'm impatient by nature." He softened his words with a grin. Her face remained stony. He released her reluctantly, immediately missing the softness of her skin beneath his. Cindy had most effectively got to him in a way no other woman had in a long, long time. He wasn't sure he liked it.

But he hadn't liked it the other way, either, when women fell too easily into his arms. Cindy required special handling, that's all. And he was convinced he was the one to provide it. Now to convince her of that fact.

His gaze roved the store and lit on a notice posted near the full-length mirror. It announced the Madronna Beach annual Blade-a-Thon, and Cindy's quest for sponsors. A pencil hung near the sponsor sheet. Parker sauntered over and added his name to the list of people pledging support.

"You training?" he asked casually when he turned back to face her.

"Every night," she said. "And I'm going to win."

"I heard the local endowment society is offering a scholarship to the winner. Trying to encourage more young people to get sponsors and go out."

"Any scholarship money would come in handy." She still looked wary, but at least she'd quit fussing with those damn shoe boxes. He chose his next words carefully.

"You practice along the seawall yet?"

"Not yet. I plan to, though."

"It's a good winding practice course," Parker said. "I'll meet you there tonight after work. Six-thirty?"

He watched her eyes narrow. "What do you mean?"

"You said you wanted to win."

"Correction. I said I *will* win."

"Positive thinking only takes a person so far. But with me as your coach—"

"I don't want a coach."

"'Course you don't. But you need one. Matter of fact, you need *me*."

"What makes you say that?"

"You happen to catch last year's race?"

"No, I was working."

"If you had, you might remember seeing me first across the finish line."

She didn't bother trying to hide her skepticism. "I didn't see your name among this year's contenders."

"That's because I decided not to enter this year. But I'll be there cheering you on." He piled on his charm carefully. Not too thick. "Hey. What have you got to lose?"

"My independence?"

"Hell, no one can take that away without your permission. I wouldn't begin to try. That's part of who you are. Frustrating most of the time. Endearing nonetheless. Very much you." He tried a half smile. No response. He didn't usually have to work this hard for a woman's attention or approval. In fact, the last time he worked this hard at a relationship… The truth hit him like a cold shower. It had been Tammy. A battle of wills over her drug use. She convinced no harm was being done. He knowing there'd be both physical and psychological repercussions. Not only was he convinced he knew better, he was convinced his love for her had the power to win. It had been a crushing defeat. Was he about to make the same mistake with Cindy?

Cindy gave him a wary glance, clearly wondering what bulldozer scheme he was working on now.

He only wanted to help. Scratch that. He wanted to see Cindy. To spend time with her, and this looked like an open opportunity. He decided to try the honest approach.

"I admit I want to see you again. And I like to help. But you make it damn difficult for anyone to offer you a hand."

Cindy appeared to weigh his words. "Help or take over?"

"Honest. Just help. It's your show all the way."

WHAT DID SHE HAVE to lose? Cindy thought later that day. She replayed Parker's words on instant replay. She'd asked the universe just this morning for help to win this race. It appeared to have sent her Parker for that express purpose.

Losing the race wasn't an option. Neither was losing herself. Which is what she was afraid would happen as long as Parker kept hanging around, insinuating himself into her life, being too darn nice to her by half.

Too patient.

Too understanding.

Too darn sexy.

So why had she agreed to his help, she wondered, as she pulled on her helmet and protective pads. She gave an extra tug to her skate laces and the nail of her index finger snapped off at the quick. She popped her finger in her mouth, instantly reminded of Parker's hot, hungry lips on hers. As she pushed herself to her feet she wished she had enough confidence to toss his coaching offer back in his face. But she wanted—make that needed—to win this prize money, and to that end she would entertain the devil himself if it helped further her goal.

She arrived at the seawall and glanced at the still-light sky. The longest day of the year, it promised to stay light for hours. Hopefully it didn't turn out to be the longest day of her life. Watching Parker step out of his truck, she felt an involuntary fluttering of her insides. Was it possible that already, in a totally roundabout way, her wish was being answered?

The darn trampoline in her stomach was affecting her balance and she felt clumsier than usual as she skated up to the truck and skidded to a stop. And the trampolining didn't settle down under Parker's easy grin. On the contrary her mouth felt dry. She was at a loss for words as she watched him don protective pads and helmet. He rapped his knuckles against her head gear. "You all warmed up?"

Too warm. Much too warm!

"You bet."

"So let's go."

Cindy sped off ahead, anxious to put distance between them and maybe, in the bargain, impress Parker with her prowess. If she put on a good enough show maybe he'd concede. Admit that she didn't really need his help.

He caught up to her far too easily, grabbed her hand and used his brakes to drag her to a stop.

"What are you doing?"

"What does it look like I'm doing? I'm practicing. What? Out with it."

"I'm not trying to be critical."

"Don't mince words with me, Parker. I can take it."

"Well, for starters, your stance is all wrong. You need to be way more crouched. Like this." He demonstrated, bent low at the waist, shoulders near level with his midsection.

"Oh," Cindy felt her confidence deflate.

"And while it's okay to take off at a dead-out sprint, I've always found it's better to pace yourself. Fake it off-line with a hard start if you like, before you pull back. Think of it like a game of cat and mouse. See who wants to take the lead. If you're smart you can position yourself for drafting and save your energy for final positioning."

"Drafting?" Cindy said.

"Yeah. Set yourself up to take full advantage of the aerodynamics of someone in front of you."

"Isn't that sort of cheating? It's not like we're geese or something."

"We can always learn from our feathered friends. And others will be doing it to you. The serious skaters. Lots of people who enter the race do it purely for the fun of the experience. Bring their kids and everything. Don't worry. The serious competitors will be out front almost from the start. And you'll be there with them.''

''What else?'' Cindy asked in a subdued voice.

''Drink water, only not too much or you might get cramps. Oh, yes, remember to watch out for the hay.''

''Hay?'' Cindy wondered if she needed her hearing checked.

''It's customary to side some of the tight course turns with bales of hay. Skaters'll run into them and you might hit loose hay on the street afterward.''

''Any other hazards I need to watch out for?''

''Gravel or sand. And paint, of course.''

''Paint?'' Cindy raised her brow for emphasis.

''Road paint. Hit a roadline the wrong way and before you know what happened you spin right out.''

Cindy sighed. ''I thought I just had to be the fastest.''

''Fast, smart and lucky.'' Parker said. ''Come on, let's see what you can do.''

This time Cindy didn't bother trying to show off. She concentrated on her stance, crouched into what felt like a most unnatural position. Maybe if she pretended she was on her bike. Yes, that felt better. As her body relaxed and settled into place she glanced over at Parker and almost preened at the approving thumbs-up he gave her. She chewed on her lower lip and followed the narrow, winding walkway.

Parker jockeyed himself in front of her and she could actually feel the aerodynamics he'd been talking about. Cool.

All of a sudden she felt a quick shock of panic rush through her. Something was wrong! Her foot shifted, seeming to possess a mind of its own. She wobbled. Her body tilted to one side as if she'd taken a sudden step down. She managed a squeaky cry. As she struggled to keep her feet in line she was aware of Parker slowing and turning in front of her. No way to avoid him. She skated right into him and bounced off. It was like hitting a cement wall. Except she didn't go down. He was positioned in such a way that he brought both of them to a stop, his arms wrapped around her waist while she gripped his forearms for balance.

"What happened?" Cindy's knees still shook, but panic had given way to awareness of the warmth of Parker's grip across her midsection.

"Looks like a blown tire."

"That's not supposed to happen, is it?"

"Says who?" Parker leaned down and checked out her skate. "That's what happened."

"What should I have done? Supposing you weren't here to catch me."

"First of all, don't panic."

"Right," Cindy muttered. Not panic? Just standing here with Parker's arms around her and knowing she had no desire to move out of his embrace was enough to send her into panic mode. Having a skate tire blow out beneath her was minor in comparison.

"You felt yourself tilt to one side, right? You simply glide on the other foot."

"Thanks." It came out gruffer than she'd intended.

But it didn't seem to faze him or make him let her go. Quite the contrary.

"My pleasure." His touch melted into pure sensuality. As his fingertips stroked the bare strip of skin on her back between her shorts and top Cindy felt a shower of sparks career through her, threatening her equilibrium. She was far more off balance than a few minutes earlier when only her foot was wobbling. She glanced up. In spite of herself she'd begun stroking his arms, enjoying the warm, hair-roughened sensation, the pull and flex of his muscles beneath her touch.

Waves of heat and longing washed over her and she had just closed her eyes against the onslaught of feelings when a stream of cold water sprayed her in the face.

Her eyes flew open in shock, riveted on Parker's equally surprised expression. From all sides the park's automatic sprinkler system showered them in cold water.

# Chapter Ten

Skin tight, saturated Lycra outlined her curves like wet paint, and as she looked down, Cindy wished she'd worn a bra. The icy shower caused her nipples to harden, brazenly outlined beneath the lime-green Lycra.

Parker was in a similar state, except on him the clingy, near-transparent T-shirt looked sexy and provocative. He was tasty enough to make a girl's mouth water, as wet cotton plastered his chest and emphasized every individual muscle ridging his shoulders and arms.

"You look like a poster pinup in one of those fanzines." She tilted her head to survey him from an angle. "I wish I had a camera."

"I wish I had a towel. Come on." Parker's hands lingered another few seconds at the small of her back, then slid around her waist, his touch as light and tantalizing as the flutter of an insect's wings. He caught her hand in his and set off, hauling her along behind him.

"Come on where?"

"My place to get dried off and changed."

"I'd rather air-dry, thanks."

"And risk getting sick right before the race? You're not thinking very clearly, darlin'."

"Did you plan that, Parker Davis?"

"Plan what? The impromptu shower? Hardly my idea of foreplay. You know what cold water does to a guy's libido, don't you?"

Cindy laughed, suddenly much more at ease. "I hope that doesn't happen during the race."

"What? A good drenching?"

"No. That I blow a tire."

"I'll check your skates over thoroughly the night before."

It turned out they were much closer to Parker's place than she'd realized and she found it a real treat to see in the daylight. She'd scarcely given her surroundings a second look when she left the other morning, there'd been too much other stuff on her mind. Today she took the time to appreciate the setting fully, privacy guaranteed by the vine-choked fences on either side of the drawbridge.

Skate wheels rang noisily as they glided across the worn wooden planks. Up close she noted how the weathered silver shingles made the boathouse look like one big piece of driftwood afloat in the Pacific. While Parker unlocked the door, Cindy unlaced her skates and took off her helmet, half gloves and pads.

"You can have first crack at the shower."

"I don't need a shower," Cindy said as she followed him inside. "Just a towel will do me fine."

"Whatever you say." Parker passed her a towel and a faded denim shirt before he gave her a gentle push in the direction of the bathroom. "Pass me out your shorts and top and I'll lay them over the deck railing to dry."

Cindy peeled off her wet shorts with difficulty and traded her top for Parker's shirt, which was long enough to qualify as a minidress on her. She folded the sleeves back and smoothed her fingers across a fabric worn incredibly soft. She buried her nose in the collar and took a deep sniff, disappointed it didn't smell like Parker. Still, she found the garment's line-dried, sun-bleached fresh scent a sexy second to her host.

She paused and gave herself a quick once-over in the mirror. As she ran her fingers through her hair in an attempt to fluff it slightly, she stuck out her tongue. It was more than a little late to start worrying about her looks. She was who she was.

The shirttails whispered against her thighs as she padded barefoot across the living room to where Parker stood on the deck. The glass-paned garage doors were rolled up into the ceiling, giving the impression that they were actually afloat, and part of her wished it were so. Just she and Parker on their own carefree voyage of discovery. She wondered how he'd react if she gave voice to her thoughts.

As if on cue Parker turned and gave her an approving look. "Lucky shirt," he said, so low-voiced she wasn't sure she'd heard correctly.

She cocked her head to one side. "The bathroom's all yours. What did you say about this shirt?"

He strolled toward her and stopped inches away to straighten the collar where it had folded under on one side, his fingers warm against her collarbone. "I said this is my lucky shirt. And it's never looked so good."

Cindy flushed. Not so much at his words, but at the husky intimacy in his voice. She gave him a playful push in an effort to keep things light between them. "You're all wet, Parker Davis."

"So I've been told before."

She felt the air between them fairly crackle with electric energy that raised the hair on her forearms and the back of her neck. So much for keeping things light. Parker was just too damn magnetic for his own good.

He clucked her lightly under the chin. "I'll be right back."

There was a promise in those words, matched by a definite promise in the way his gaze lingered on hers.

Cindy rested her forearms on the deck rail and drank in the aromatic sea air as she listened to the rhythmic slap of the waves against the pilings.

"I could live here." She whispered the words to herself, amazed by the pervading sense of peace that stole through her. The sky was ablaze with a cacophony of colors, streaks of gold, pink, teal and mauve. As if a child, in gay abandon, had ravaged her box of watercolors.

She sensed rather than heard Parker behind her.

That darn electricity again. Slowly she turned. He wore a terry robe and, unless she missed her guess, little else. A towel was slung over one shoulder. His hair was still damp, gleaming almost black in the sunset. He carried a bottle of wine and two glasses, which he placed next to her elbow on the deck rail.

"I could stand here for hours. In fact, I often do," he said as he rubbed at his wet hair with the towel. Cindy's gaze remained riveted on two distracting droplets of water nestled in the tangle of dark chest hair peeping from the neckline of his robe.

"Do you have any idea how lucky you are?"

He gave her a long, significant look that led her to suspect they were talking about two entirely different things. "I'm just starting to appreciate my good fortune all over again."

Silence stretched taut between them, one of those lulls that between other people might have felt uncomfortable and seen each of them leaping in to try to fill the void. But from the first, in Parker's presence, Cindy felt no need for idle chatter.

She watched him open the wine, a task he performed as expertly as he did everything. He splashed the liquid into long-stemmed glassware, a shimmer of ruby red that matched the blazing sky.

Cindy swirled and took an appreciative sniff.

"It's a merlot from one of the small wineries up the coast," Parker said.

She took a sip. The wine slid like velvet across her tongue. "It's delicious." Cindy studied the contents of her glass, then glanced sideways at Parker. "When

I started waitressing, I was lucky to land a boss who believed in educating his staff about wines. He maintained we couldn't sell what we didn't know, and once a week after work, he'd sit us down to study a different wine-making region.'' She laughed. ''It was my favorite part of the job. Poor man was quite upset to learn his keenest pupil was underage.''

''I hope he didn't fire you.''

''On the contrary, he wangled me some official-looking ID.'' She smiled sadly. ''He was a terrific guy. Unfortunately he liked his French food way too much, and all the red wine in the restaurant cellars couldn't keep his arteries clear. He keeled over a year later from a massive coronary.''

''Funny, the people who cycle in and out of our lives, usually for a reason we aren't even aware of at the time.''

His eyes and his voice seemed to have crept backward into the past. Was he thinking about Tammy? She felt an uncomfortable pinprick of awareness. It made no sense, resenting his thoughts about another woman when he was with her. Still, Cindy couldn't stop herself from taking a step closer. ''Why do you think you cycled into my life when you did?''

''Possibly for no other reason than to share this sunset, this moment with you tonight.'' His words sent something warm rushing through her veins. She told herself not to panic, to take the lesson life was right now willing to offer her, to experience, to learn.

''Does that mean, once the sun has set, our association is ended?''

"Heck, no. Not till you cross that finish line this weekend."

"Okay, coach." She plunged in. "And why am I in your life?"

"I think maybe you're here to serve as a reminder."

"A reminder of what?"

Parker reached out and tucked a strand of hair behind her ear. She shivered as the pads of his fingers brushed the curve of her lobe. "A reminder of life's simple pleasures. Good wine. Gracious company."

"The world's best view."

"The world's best view," Parker echoed. But he was gazing at her as he said it, and the look in his eyes sent a fresh wave of heat and desire rippling through her.

Cradling the bowl of her wineglass in both hands she raised it to her lips.

"Don't do that." Parker stopped her with a light touch to the back of her hand.

"What?"

"Always hold your wineglass by the stem. That way your body heat doesn't alter the wine's temperature."

She glanced at the wineglass. Her body heat was enough to set it aboil. "I knew that," Cindy said softly. "I just needed something to hold on to."

Parker took the glass from her hand and set it on the rail next to his.

"What's wrong with holding on to me?"

"Everything," Cindy said.

"You'll need to be a bit more specific than that."

"I'm afraid."

"Didn't we already work through your fears?"

"This is a new one."

"You're not afraid of me?"

"Of course not. I'm afraid that if I start holding on to you, I'll never let go. And I'll forget how to do things for myself."

He stroked her chin with the back of his hand. "Did you ever hear that poem about the best friend?"

Cindy shook her head.

"I can't remember, exactly. But it goes something along the lines of 'A best friend is someone who knows the song you sing in your heart, and sings it for you when you forget the words.'" Cindy moistened her lips, aware she had a lump the size of a basketball lodged in her throat. She blinked rapidly, afraid if she didn't a lone tear might escape.

"I've never had a best friend like that."

"I beg to differ. You might not be aware of it. You do your darnedest to keep that song a secret. But a best friend knows all."

"I don't want that kind of a best friend." Cindy squared her shoulders. Felt her old resolve, her old armor resurfacing to protect her. How had that happened? For a minute there she had almost lost it. Had almost melted into Parker's arms. Sobbed out all her fears and insecurities and closely guarded secrets like some weak, pathetic, friendless little waif.

She was none of those things. She was strong. Focused. Capable. And most of all, a loner.

She turned away and plucked her Lycra outfit from the rail. "I'll go get changed. Thanks for the wine. And the lesson."

Parker was hardly surprised when she retreated. He still felt like he was coaxing a wild creature to get close, baby step by baby step. Cindy wasn't ready yet to eat out of his hand. She was still wary. Yet she claimed to feel safe with him. She knew he wouldn't force himself on her the way that lout Lowther had done. And when she had come to him, warm and willing and on her terms, it had been an unforgettable moment.

Women. He shook his head and set to the immediate task of fixing her blown tire. They skated back to his truck in mutual silence, almost as if each realized they had possibly revealed too much to the other.

Still, he determined to drive Cindy home and, half expecting her to fight him on it, was pleasantly surprised when she made no protest. Maybe she was as tired out as he was. He pulled up around back of her apartment and left the motor idling, just so she wouldn't think he expected her to ask him in.

"Same time, same place tomorrow?"

He watched a haze of hesitancy cloud her eyes. "You don't have to, Parker. It's no skin off your nose whether I win or not."

"I'm egotistical enough to think the right coach can make a difference. I pray you don't shatter my illusions now."

His words got a smile, which was exactly what

he'd hoped. Keep things light. Lord knew it didn't take much in the way of sudden moves to send Cinderella bolting.

"Tomorrow, then."

He sat in the truck till she was safely inside and he saw her kitchen light go on. Then he dashed home and read up on the latest techniques so he could be the well-informed coach she deserved. Not just some guy blowing smoke in order to spend time in her company.

"TELL ME AGAIN JUST WHY I'm wearing this blindfold?"

Marissa giggled. They were in a moving vehicle, which meant her friend had an accomplice. Cindy was praying it wasn't Parker, although she couldn't say why, exactly. Maybe she liked keeping him safely at arm's length. And if he made friends with Marissa...

She heard gears grind as they slowed to a stop, then sped up again. They were heading southwest was her guess. But she'd never driven around blindfolded before.

"I know you packed a towel. I heard you rummaging in the bathroom."

"Why don't you like surprises?" Marissa said.

"No control," was Cindy's automatic response. Truth was, she'd never been on the receiving end of a surprise. They hadn't been Sheri's forte. Her mother had been forthright to a fault. No tooth fairy. No Santa Claus or Easter Bunny. Sheri never kept a thing from her daughter, except of course the most important thing. The identity of Cindy's father.

And funny, learning from Maude the story of her father and his demise had made no difference in how she perceived herself, although it afforded her a different way of looking at her mother.

"Hey, I smell the ocean," Cindy said as the vehicle braked to a stop. "Are we close to the pier?"

"You're a tough one to surprise," Marissa said, pulling the scarf away from Cindy's face.

Cindy blinked in the bright sunlight. "Look at that," she crowed. They were at a boat rental not all that far from the pier. In Tom's van, she was pleased to note, not Parker's truck.

"How'd she sucker you in?" she asked Tom as he wheeled into a parking spot.

Tom reddened. "What can I say? Your friend has quite a way about her."

"We're going kayaking," Marissa said cheerfully. "I packed a picnic and Tom knows this great spot and—"

"Absolutely not!" Cindy thundered. "It's way too dangerous." She appealed to Tom. Surely he'd have better sense. "Plus, you're afraid of the ocean."

Marissa gave Cindy a haughty stare. "You've always told me how fabulous kayaking is. Skimming across the water like a gull."

"The kayak could tip. Anything could happen."

"You ever tip over a kayak, Cin? What about you, Tom?"

Both of them shook their heads.

"It's time I met my fears head-on," Marissa said. "That way they won't have control of me or my life. Besides, Tom's here if anything happens."

"Marissa, I can't believe you're willing to put all your trust in the hands of others."

"It feels good," Marissa said, adding pointedly, "You ought to give it a try sometime. You were against me taking up riding again, if memory serves me rightly, yet it's been the best thing I've done for myself in years. Don't you agree?"

"Agreed," Cindy said reluctantly.

Marissa always had a ready response. And clearly, in this instance at least, there was no point in going up against her. Better to go along with her and pray nothing untoward happened.

They boarded from shore. Tom waded in with Marissa and, with Cindy holding the kayak steady, settled her in the front of the double kayak. At least Marissa wasn't insisting on having her own single. Cindy was also relieved to note he passed on skirting Marissa in. Still against her better judgment, Cindy climbed into her rented single and the three of them started off, staying close to shore.

It was a flat, calm day. No surfers dotted the sun-shimmered expanse. As she paddled, Cindy felt herself relax the way she always did on the water. The smell. The sound. The motion. It was a balm for her frazzled senses.

She glanced at Marissa, who was clearly enchanted, all her fear of the vast expanse of water forgotten as she exclaimed over the brightly colored starfish clinging to the rocks. Or the curious seal whose head surfaced six feet away.

"Oh, look! Isn't he cute?"

"Not if you were fishing and he stole your bait," Tom said with a good-natured grin.

Marissa addressed Cindy. "I see now why you love to kayak. The space is boundless."

They skimmed along in silence, heading south. Cindy could feel the warmth of the sun on her right arm and shoulder.

"Oh, look." Marissa pointed with her paddle. "Isn't that Parker?"

It was indeed, Cindy realized with a painful twist to her insides. How could she not have realized where they were headed?

"Yoo-hoo, Parker." Marissa raised her paddle like a flagpole as Tom steered their kayak up to Parker's deck.

"Hey!" Parker grinned over the rail at them. Did Cindy only imagine it, or did his gaze find and dismiss her in less time than it took to blink? "This looks like trouble."

"Want to find trouble with us?" Marissa asked. "I packed a *huge* picnic."

"What man can refuse an offer like that, specially when it includes the company of two beautiful women? Give me five minutes."

Cindy paddled aimlessly in circles, aware of the happy glow in her best friend's eyes as Marissa chattered to Tom, and she tried to swallow her resentment. She wanted to be the one responsible for Marissa's animation, to help her conquer her fears. Instead, it had taken this strong, silent he-man to recognize and respond to what Marissa needed.

Cindy was instantly ashamed. Tom was a fine man. She'd taken to him instantly. And Marissa was entitled to be happy. No one deserved it more.

"Where we headed?" Parker had joined them so silently she wasn't aware of his presence till he spoke.

"I thought Race Rocks park. There's a picnic site there, not usually too much traffic."

"Perfect." Parker kayaked as expertly as he did everything, Cindy was quick to note. He'd probably had lessons at some ritzy summer camp when he was a kid, unlike her, who had learned in a leaky home-made version fashioned by one of Sheri's many boy-friends.

"What a great idea," Parker said as he drew abreast of her and kept pace, leaving Tom and Marissa to set their own speed. "It's not often this flat calm."

Cindy glanced over her shoulder to the double kayak. "I'm worried about Rissa. What if something happens?"

"Tom won't let anything happen to your friend, Cindy. You can count on that."

"Sometimes things happen that are beyond our control."

"What?" Parker asked. "What has ever happened that you couldn't control?"

*Falling for you,* Cindy thought, but she couldn't

say that out loud. "Losing that shoe, and all the hassle getting it back," she said.

"Yet everything turned out all right in the end," Parker said cheerfully.

"Only with your help," Cindy said. "Otherwise, who knows how it might have turned out?"

"You don't like accepting help, do you?" Parker said.

"Not a bit," Cindy said. "I hate being beholden."

"Did you ever consider what an act of selfishness that is? People feel good when they lend a hand, and you spend most of your days denying them that good feeling."

"You and I see the world differently, Parker. It doesn't necessarily mean one's right and one's wrong. They're just different perspectives." Then she put on a surge of speed and pulled ahead of him, hoping he'd take the hint and leave her be.

She reached the marine park first. More like Parker let her get there ahead of him. If he'd so chosen he could have beaten her by a mile. She beached her canoe and watched the others approach. Marissa was laughing at something Tom said. Up close her cheeks were starting to pinken. Cindy made a mental note to make sure she was wearing sunscreen. She waded out and pulled the double kayak onto shore. Parker, she knew, was more than capable of taking care of himself.

"If you preferred I not join you, you ought to have said something at the time," Parker told Cindy, out of earshot of the others, as he secured his kayak on the shore next to hers.

Tom was carrying Marissa to a picnic table, leaving Cindy and Parker to drag the soft-sided cooler and food backpack out of the dry-hold.

"Why would I mind?" Cindy slung the pack onto her shoulders.

"Beats me," Parker said. "But you've barely spared me a look or a word."

"Don't take it seriously. I've some things on my mind."

"Share with me." He touched her in spite of swearing he wasn't going to; he couldn't seem to help himself. It was just a light caress to the forearm, but it was like petting a wild creature. You never knew if they'd accept the touch or lash out.

"Why should I make you privy to my innermost thoughts?"

"It's called communication. And if you try it, you might find you like it."

"I never considered bullying in the same class as communication."

"Bullying?" Parker felt stung by her words. "I don't bully. I was invited here today."

"I'm not talking about today," Cindy said. "I'm talking about how you showed up to help me move. And how, in spite of my initial refusal, you insisted on being my coach. Even picking out your sister's footwear. Making decisions for everyone else, just because you feel you're right."

Parker closed his mouth on his initial response. To

defend himself. Because in spite of everything, he recognized the ring of truth to her words.

"Something wrong with trying to lend a hand?" he asked quietly.

"Not a thing. But imposing your will on others, even if you are right, and they're wrong is. People have to do things for themselves."

He looked totally shocked. "Hey!" Cindy said. This time she touched him, laid her hand against his shoulder. "It's not that tragic. You're hardly the only guilty party." She waved a hand to where Tom and Marissa sat at the picnic table, heads so close they practically touched, engrossed in just the two of them.

"I keep trying to impose my will on Marissa. Thinking I know best. She's forever reminding me she's a grown-up and entitled to make her own choices. Her own way." She gave a heavy sigh, then surprised Parker by pressing a quick kiss to his cheek.

"What's that for?"

"I would have given my right arm to see Marissa as happy as she is today. Yet it took Tom. And since you introduced him to me…"

"Might I remind you? Those two met all by themselves. Neither of us had a thing to do with it."

"That's right," Cindy said. "I'd forgotten. So maybe it was just destiny after all."

"We can't control nearly as much as we think we can. In spite of what we think."

"Hey, you two," Marissa called. "Hustle that food over here. I'm starving."

As Marissa got out the picnic foods, she snuck covert glances at Cindy and Parker, relieved by the absence of tension she'd sensed earlier. She knew Cindy's prickly exterior masked a vulnerable soft heart. She'd always known it would take a very special man to scale past that protective mantle.

Tom reached across the table and stroked the back of her hand. She flipped her hand over and linked her fingers through his. No words were necessary. Her heart felt full to the bursting point. Now that she'd met Tom she wanted everyone she cared about to be as happy as she was.

She hadn't always trusted the right people in her life, but she'd never given up. It had been easy to take a risk today, to conquer her fears. To trust Tom. Cindy's fears of love and hurt and rejection ran far deeper.

"This is my very own fried chicken recipe," she said. "And my roast potato and green bean salad."

"Beautiful and she cooks, too," Tom said. Marissa felt herself flush with pleasure at his words.

"It's a treat having someone to cook for for a change. My kitchen's well set up for it, but lots of days it hardly seems worth the bother."

"Next time it's my turn to cook," Tom said. "You can be my guest."

"I'd love that. You hear that, Cin? Tom just invited all of us to his place for a meal."

Parker choked on a laugh. "I heard him invite you, Marissa. He might not appreciate the rest of us tagging along."

Marissa's color deepened. "Is that right, Tom? Dinner for two?"

"Something like that," Tom muttered, clearly embarrassed. "The rest of you are welcome, too, of course."

"Well, I don't cook," Cindy said, reaching for a homemade biscuit. "So I love it when someone else takes over."

"Could have fooled me," Parker said, low-voiced.

Cindy shot him a look that plainly said she didn't care to hear any more on that particular topic. She jumped up and fetched cans of iced tea, which she passed around the table.

"I made lemon loaf and oatmeal chocolate chip cookies for dessert."

Marissa's words were greeted with a round of groans.

"I think we're all stuffed. Let's save them for later. Come on, Cindy." Parker rose and started to gather up the dishes. "Marissa cooked, so it's our job to go wash up."

Cindy shot him a puzzled glance but obediently rose and started to gather up empty salad bowls and serving utensils. Tom and Marissa seemed oblivious to their departure.

"I thought we should give those two some time alone," Parker said.

"So it was more than a sudden surge of domesticity on your part?"

"You might recall, I can be extremely domestic," Parker said. "You just didn't stick around long enough to fully appreciate it. Mom raised Lisa and I equal.'' They reached the parks board water tap and he put down his bundle of dishes, claimed Cindy's from her and added them to the pile. He took her into his arms and held her shoulders gently as she faced him.

''What?''

''I just wanted to tell you you're right about what you said earlier. I do kind of bulldoze in there, don't I?''

''It's not as if it's not well-intentioned,'' Cindy said. ''But not everyone appreciates being strong-armed.''

''I still would like to coach you for the race,'' Parker said. ''But only if you agree of your own free will.''

''I appreciate that,'' Cindy said. ''And accept your kind offer.''

His hands slid from her shoulders to her neck to cup her jaw with the utmost gentleness. ''I've had this urge all day to kiss you.''

Cindy swallowed vigorously, then nodded. ''We have to find some way to occupy ourselves while we leave Tom and Marissa to their own devices.''

''We do indeed. As long as you're sure you don't mind that Marissa invited me along.''

Cindy dampened her lips with the tip of her tongue. ''Well you did save me from the uncomfortable feeling of being the third wheel around those two.''

''Nothing worse than feeling like a third wheel. Your presence saved me at Bambi's wedding.''

"So we're even," Cindy said.

Parker released her with mock exasperation. "What is this hang-up you have about being even? What makes you think someone is out there keeping score?"

"You're right," Cindy said, moving close to him in a bold move that surprised even her. Usually she was far too afraid of being rejected. "No one's keeping score." She realized suddenly that pushing Parker away was infinitely worse. What if she pushed him away for good?

"That's better." He tilted her chin up, drew her near with his free hand against her back, and settled his mouth atop hers.

Cindy sighed at the rightness of melting into his arms as their lips renewed their previous acquaintance. He was a divine kisser, just the right amount of pressure and damp heat, coupled with a talented tongue that welcomed hers, as its knowing moves inflamed her senses.

When he eventually ended the kiss, they were both breathing heavily, but she wasn't ready for it to be over. Boldly she cupped his head between her hands, urging his mouth back for further mating with hers. His hands settled on her hips, positioning them against his. She allowed her hands free exploration up the T-shirt-clad contours of his chest, chafing at the confines of clothing between them.

"Cindy, I—" He drew her hands away and kept them loosely clasped with his, as if he couldn't take much more touching, yet couldn't bear to let her go.

Whatever he was going to say was interrupted by the vibration of his cell phone on his belt.

He flashed her a helpless look as he answered it.

"Parker here. Conny? Slow down. Take a breath. Where? I'll be there as quickly as I can."

His look was tinged with regret, but she knew what he was going to say even before he spoke.

"I'm sorry. I have to go."

"It's all right," Cindy said. "Don't let me stop you."

"Sorry to leave you with all the dishes."

"Don't be silly," Cindy said. "Go do what you have to do."

"Yeah," Parker said over his shoulder. She watched his stride lengthen to a near run as he approached Marissa and Tom, then sprinted for his kayak.

She hadn't been rejected, Cindy told herself. This wasn't abandonment she felt. Someone named Connie had a prior claim on him, that's all. Why would she expect to have things any other way?

## *Chapter Eleven*

They practiced every night for the rest of the week with no more dousings or excuses to go to his place. The day before the race he could tell Cindy was a whole lot more comfortable around him. Certainly not dependent on him; that wouldn't be her style. But she didn't dance away when he adjusted her pads and tightened her laces, and even managed to laugh at his jokes without sounding forced.

A couple of times she actually reached for him, her light touch catching his attention. Her hand on his arm, her fingers brushing his shoulder. Her gaze holding his. He liked it.

"You won't be needing these tonight." He tossed her skates in the back seat of the Mustang.

"What do you mean?"

He opened the passenger door and, one hand beneath her elbow, nudged her into the car. He didn't believe she'd actually turn tail and run, but her eyes on his were brimming with uncertainty. She wanted to trust him, but as usual the brakes were full on.

He reached for his sunglasses and waited till the

car was in gear before he answered. "You've trained hard. It's time now to let up. To have some fun."

"Fun?" Cindy squeaked. "Are you crazy? The race is tomorrow. This is my last chance to practice." She had one hand on the door handle, as if she might fling it open and hurl herself from the car.

"Cindy, I'm your coach. You've listened to me all week. Tonight I'm telling you, you're as ready as you'll ever be. You need to give your mind and your body a rest."

"So what do you propose?"

"I thought we'd rent a couple of horses from a guy I know and take a ride through the hills."

"Trail riding?"

"Yeah. I don't know if you ride."

"Are you kidding? I love to ride," Cindy said. "I just haven't had much opportunity."

"Great." Parker bit back a self-satisfied smile. Score one more for the gods of wisdom who had gifted him with this latest scheme to help Cindy relax in his company, worlds away from distractions of everyday life.

They reached the stable in short order and found their horses saddled and ready.

"What's that you've got there?" Cindy asked as he stuffed a few things into his saddlebag. She was already mounted on Caramel Corn, a sturdy yet pretty mare whose color gave her her name, and to his eye she appeared to be as natural in the saddle as anyplace else he'd seen her. Cindy and her gift of fit-right-in.

"A few necessities," Parker said as he swung himself into the saddle. Lucky Dollar and he were old friends, and the horse responded to him so well it almost seemed to read his mind. Together they started for the hills.

"Necessities like what?"

"Necessities such as brie, wine and a fresh baguette."

He heard the sounds of her soft, muffled laughter as Caramel Corn pulled up abreast of Lucky Dollar. "Here I was expecting to hear you say a first aid kit."

"You planning to hurt yourself?"

"Nope, but the thought crossed my mind, just in case you're planning to try anything, that bandages might be a good idea." Her words were softened by the laughter in her voice.

He gave her a slow, leisurely perusal, and relished the way she colored slightly under his gaze.

"That shirt of yours would make a nifty sling. Might be worth a broken arm to see what you're wearing underneath."

Cindy sputtered indignantly but didn't snap back with a barbed retort. Instead, she put her heels to Caramel's flanks and took off ahead of him in a cloud of dust.

He caught up to her in a matter of minutes. "Caramel's happier when Lucky's in the lead."

She shot him a brazen look. "Now, why would that be?"

"Some folks just happen to be natural-born leaders. Animals, too."

"I never believed that. I think everyone has an abil-

ity to do what needs doing. Some might just have to
work a little harder than others to tap into that power,
is all.''

He leaned across his saddle toward her. ''Quit
keeping me at arm's length, Cinderella. It's not a
comfortable distance for me.''

''Me, neither,'' Cindy said. ''It's much too close.''

Her words didn't faze him in the least. ''We'll see
about that. But since this is supposed to be relaxing
for you and take your mind off tomorrow's race, can
Lucky and I please lead the way?''

''If you must.''

The real reason Parker wanted to take the lead was
because he knew exactly where they were headed.
Their destination was a spot he'd discovered one time
on his own, a rocky precipice that from a distance
appeared inaccessible. But he'd persevered and, with
Lucky's help, had found a well-disguised trail to the
top, where a panoramic vista spread for miles in all
directions. To find himself there at sunset in the company of a special someone was a long-held fantasy of
his. Till now, he'd never wanted to turn it into a reality, always afraid it would disappoint. He had a feeling Cindy's reaction would prove anything but a let-
down.

In spite of her bluster Cindy was quite content to
have Caramel fall into lead behind Lucky. She'd
never ridden in these parts before and was relishing
the experience. Scrub vegetation clung precariously
to rocky crevices. The ground beneath the horse's
hooves was tinder dry and it amazed her that this

much vegetation managed to exist. The surrounding boulders held the day's heat so even the breeze, riffling through her hair, was warm. Sultry. Daytime would be too hot up here, like a blast furnace, but with the sun riding low in the west the temperature was utterly perfect. A warm and comfortable cocoon, freshened by the breeze. Perfect, just like everything Parker planned, damn him. The man truly had a gift.

Several, in fact. Right now she was enjoying the view in front of her, man and beast fused into one efficient unit. Ever since their first meeting Parker had continued to be full of surprises, and she had a feeling that tonight would be little different.

How was it that he'd managed to stay single? She would have expected some lucky, determined woman to have scooped him up long ago, for he was thoughtful, generous and easy to look at. He had to be near thirty and she'd heard that men had biological clocks, the need to nest and procreate, the same as women. So why wasn't he with someone? Unless, in spite of everything he said, he was still carrying a whopper of a torch for Tammy.

"How come you never married?" The question was blurted from her lips before she could stop it.

Lucky stopped on a dime, as if he was shocked by her nerve. Parker turned in the saddle.

"Did I hear you right?"

"Yeah," Cindy said. "Chalk it up to me being uncharacteristically direct."

Parker laughed. "I think maybe I'm being a bad influence." He sobered. "As far as I'm concerned there's only one reason a man and woman ought to make that kind of commitment. Because they want to spend every last one of their tomorrows together.''

''I just wondered, is all. I mean you are getting of an age.''

''Yeah, just about left on the shelf,'' Parker agreed with a rueful grin. ''But I'd rather be alone than with the wrong person. And I've met my share of those who clearly aren't the right one.''

''Don't give up,'' Cindy said breezily. ''I'm sure she'll come along eventually.''

''I'm counting on it,'' Parker said. ''I'm too nice of a guy to remain a bachelor.''

Nice, Cindy conceded. Dangerously so. Darn sexy, too. She was conscious of his musky male odor, wafting her way. The swaying motion of the horse beneath her haunches wasn't helping. It seemed to be helping shake loose more than a few of those electric-charged feelings that surfaced exclusively in Parker's presence.

Her bones and muscles felt supple and fluid, almost as if she and the horse were one in the heat, the scenery, the motion. Cindy blinked. She felt light-headed. Had they climbed that high? Maybe it was the altitude, having an adverse effect on her.

''Oh, my word, just look at that crow's nest. What the view must be from up there.''

Parker followed her gaze. Was that a self-satisfied smirk on his lips. Now what? Cindy got the distinct feeling she'd played right into his hands.

''That's where we're headed.''

"How can we? It appears inaccessible."

"You know how looks can be deceiving."

Can't they just? Cindy thought. Nothing in Parker's physical appearance had prepared her for his thoughtful caring ways. He looked as if he'd been spoiled by the silver spoon, one to take each and every piece of good luck for granted, but she knew him well enough to know he was anything but.

Parker and Lucky led the way up a well-disguised switchback trail. The way was narrow and steep and a couple of times Caramel's hooves slid on the crumbly dust.

"Easy, girl." Cindy wondered if she was talking to the horse or herself. "The boys know where they're going."

Caramel obviously trusted Lucky, for the mare followed pluckily and Cindy envied the animal that simple trust. How uncomplicated it must be to trust instinctively, rather than find oneself constantly second-guessing and overanalyzing the way she did. She sighed, well aware it was the only way she'd survived being on her own. She'd never known the luxury of blind trust.

THEIR ASCENT SEEMED to last forever, but eventually they reached the pinnacle and Cindy sucked in her breath. The countryside unfurled before them, a 360-degree view. The ocean shimmered miles to the west, glistening with the fire of the setting sun that rendered the sky ablaze. Cindy felt as if she, too, was aflame, engulfed in the magic and the splendor of the vista, where shadowy mountain crags watched them from all sides like indulgent guardians.

"I feel so small," Cindy said.

"Why are you whispering?"

"I feel like we shouldn't be here. Like we don't belong. Any minute now the gods will realize we're trespassing. A huge hand will reach from the sky, pluck us up like tiny toy soldiers and set us down below where we belong."

"It's humbling, all right." But there was nothing humble in the self-satisfied smile Parker sent her way.

"You don't look suitably humbled."

"What do you mean?" He pulled his Stetson from his head and placed it over his heart. "I'm just a simple country boy, in awe of my surroundings."

"You've never been in awe of anything in your entire life, Parker Davis." As she spoke Cindy dismounted and stretched.

"Not true."

"You're sure this is good for me? All these new muscles I'm using. What if they're sore tomorrow? Too sore for me to race?"

Parker dismounted and swaggered toward her. There was no other way to describe his rolling walk, hips thrust aggressively forward. Her mouth went dry in anticipation, knowing what was about to come next.

He touched her with all the intimacy of a life-long lover. A gentle, soothing movement that slid from her shoulders to her hips like a cascade of running water. "I'll give you a massage later."

"That won't be necessary." She felt as stiff as she knew she sounded. Reminded herself again of how Parker took certain things for granted.

"Hang 'necessary.' I'm thinking it might be a whole lot of fun. Don't tell me you didn't enjoy it last time I gave you a massage."

It was the first time he'd spoken of that night at her new apartment. The liberties he had taken and she had allowed. She'd tried to pretend it never happened. To act as if that night at his place after the wedding was their first intimate encounter.

She opted to brazen her way through. "What do you want, Parker?"

"Nothing much. Except have you throw down your sword and shield. Meet me here unarmed."

"What are you talking about?"

"You know darn well what I'm talking about. You don't need defense tactics around me, Cin. We've been over this ground before." As he spoke his hands were busy tunneling through her hair, eliciting the most delicious response from her scalp. A response that spread like heated honey through the rest of her.

"How do you know what I need?"

"Instinct." His lips claimed hers as if he owned them, and Cindy melted into his arms.

Parker felt his entire body begin to tremble, starting with the soles of his feet and working upward. That Cindy could have such an effect with just one little kiss....

Except it wasn't little. The kiss they shared was big and lush and powerful. Heat and light sparked a primal hunger that spoke to his maleness the same as this woman, whose soul spoke to his.

He ended the embrace gently and put her from him, leaving his arm looped across her shoulder. He couldn't bear to deny himself the pleasure of touching her, but if he touched her much more he was going to lose it.

"Let's sit over here. I'll open the wine."

She slanted him a puzzled glance and he knew what she was thinking. First he'd pulled her into his arms as if he'd never let her go. Yet the second he felt her start to go all soft and responsive he pulled back. Mixed signals, from his brain to hers.

He wanted her. But he wanted her to want him with equal fervor, not just submit because she was caught up in the mood or the moment. He wanted her to want him with a passion that equalled his. He wanted her to want him because he was as necessary to her as water or air. And if he couldn't have her that way, he wouldn't have her at all.

He spread a blanket on the ground, opened the wine and the brie and ripped off a chunk of bread, gnawing on it as if he was starving. Truth told he was starving for Cindy. But he needed all of her, and he didn't think she was ready to give over.

"Something about this spot reminds me of a time when I was little," Cindy said. "One of Sheri's boyfriends was a self-proclaimed preacher. He sure could talk a good talk. One weekend we loaded up the bus and went off into the hills someplace, to what looked like a natural chapel carved out of the hills. Bourne, that was his name, preached and prayed all day and into the night. It was mesmerizing. Hundreds of people were there, hanging on his every word. They just kept pouring in, I don't know where from. At one point near sunset this huge rainbow prism shone through a gap in the rocks. It was magnified. I felt as if I could reach out and touch it. The crowd went wild. I thought I had experienced this side of heaven. Then I heard Sheri and Bourne talking the next day. It was a trick with a crystal and a mirror. From that day forward, I never took anything at face value again.''

"You lost your innocence." Parker was unable to stop himself from touching her. First he rubbed her shoulders. Then stroked her arms, his callused fingertips running across the creamy satin of her skin. He took a deep breath. Saturated his senses with her fragrance and felt himself ache with wanting.

She gestured to the panorama visible below them. "Is this the same? An illusion you achieved with smoke and mirrors? Or the real thing."

"It's as real as I am."

Cindy curled herself against him. "Then you've just given me back a most precious gift. Something I thought I'd lost forever."

"What's that?"

"You've given me back my innocence. My belief in the world."

"You never lost that. It was just difficult for you to recognize."

Cindy shifted in his arms till she was sprawled

across him in a totally provocative way. He could feel her soft female parts fueling his own carefully banked passion. ''Ever make love during the sunset?''

He didn't answer. He couldn't. As she spoke she busied herself with the buttons on his shirt, and the second they were unfastened her hot, probing tongue darted across his chest. Inside and out, his body ached in more ways than he would have thought possible.

As if she'd been doing it all her life she unfastened his belt and unzipped his jeans to find him hard and hot and ready for her. He sucked in his breath and called on every ounce of self-control he possessed to take it slow. To savor the anticipation. Perspiration sheened his skin and he trembled anew as she knelt before him. Slowly she unfastened her shirt and let it slide from her shoulders. Inch by tantalizing inch her body came to view, awash with the most incredible shades of rosy pink and orange gold from the sunset. Parker felt the overwhelming need to consume her. Before she consumed him.

He ached. He burned. He pulled her to him in a move more desperate than any he'd ever known. The way a drowning man would grab for a lifeline.

She came to him. His goddess. His queen. Her flesh joined his, their souls fused, and in the embers of the sunset they reached the unreachable pinnacle far above their own.

Parker held her afterward, unable to let her go, afraid to hang on because to hang on to her would take her away from him more surely than anything he might do. And as she nestled against him in serene contentment he recalled her earlier words to him and knew them to be true. "Never try to tame something wild."

THE BLADE-A-THON course comprised thirteen winding, hilly miles of Madronna Beach outskirts, beginning and ending at the downtown park. He had driven her along the route several times, pointing out the logical spots to try to draft, the best places to pass, as well as the optimum stretches to go hell-bent for victory, and she listened with all the serious intensity he'd come to expect from her. The Cindy he knew did nothing by half measures. Her life continued to be an all-or-nothing proposition. And he wanted her all.

The race route was closed to traffic, manned by dozens of volunteers in reflective traffic-safety vests. The competitors pinned on their numbers and hugged the starting line, hundreds of them, from towns up and down the coast. Parker knew the majority of the racers were here not only for the challenge, but for the party after.

Cindy was eye-catching in her lime-sherbet-colored outfit, and as he listened for the starter's gun he realized he was more keyed-up than last year when he'd been one of the competitors. He felt as if more than just a race was being decided here and now today. Cindy's standing at the finish line stood directly linked to her standing with him. If she won the race, he won the girl.

Stupid logic.

It made no sense at all. And yet he couldn't shake off the thought.

Had he ever been this nervous?

He nodded in approval as Cindy took up a proper stance. She led off at a dead-out sprint, then cat-and-moused the way he'd coached her. He watched till she was out of sight, then he made his way around the park to the finish line.

He was nowhere near the first spectator on scene, but one person he hadn't expected to see was Cindy's mother, Sheri, with the boyfriend, Frank, in tow. She recognized him and waved him over.

"How did you know Cindy would be racing today?"

Sheri forced a laugh. "Believe it or not she called me up and asked me to sponsor her."

"That sounds promising."

"And proves sometimes prayers do get answered. She's barely spoken to me in years. But Frank figured it was her way of extending the olive branch. Inviting me back into her life." Sheri squinted toward the finish line. "You think she has a chance?"

"You know how determined Cindy can be once she sets her mind a certain way. Nothing gets in her road."

"I also know what she's like when things don't turn out quite the way she thinks they should."

"She'll be disappointed if she doesn't finish first. But she'll just dust herself off and find some other brass ring to jump at."

Sheri gave him a shrewd look. "Be careful. Sounds

as if you know Cindy better than Cindy knows Cindy.''

"Why do you say 'be careful?'"

"If she even suspects just how well you have her pegged, she'll bolt."

Wasn't that just the truth? Parker thought. "Fortunately, I know her well enough to know that as well."

Sheri nodded. "I wish you luck. 'Cause if she ever even gets a whiff of someone she suspects doing her wrong, even with the best of intentions, she will never forget. And guaranteed to never forgive."

"She's a pretty black-and-white kind of girl, all right."

Sheri gave him a look positively glowing with motherly pride. "And no matter how thorny she can pretend to be, she's worth cultivating."

"I know that, too," Parker said.

# Chapter Twelve

At first Cindy was unable to identify the myriad of feelings that swept through her. All she knew was that as she pushed her body to the limits of her endurance she was experiencing something far beyond the ordinary. Something without her usual driven desperation. That's when it hit. For the first time in her life she was awash with self-confidence and optimism. Not arrogance. Not cocky overconfidence. Just a calm serenity she found both new and awe-inspiring.

Times past she'd forced herself to leap at every challenge, regardless of whether she flew or fell. Forced herself to keep on. To never give up. Today an entirely different surge of energy propelled her forward; she felt she couldn't fail.

Where did such feelings spring from? Could this be what separated the winners from the almost-ran? Maybe people like Parker were born with this birthright, leaving the rest of the populace to scramble around and hope to discover it. Buoyant confidence fueled her limbs: a gift. Victory was hers. Vet school as good as done. Her future set.

As she felt herself pull near the front of the competitors she realized that desperation might work to propel one along short-term. For the long haul, a girl required far more in the way of staying power. In life, as in this race, she needed to pay more attention to the strategy of those around her.

She'd always barreled through life focused solely on the finish line, missing out on the sights along the way. Parker had changed all that. Shown her a different way, a place where the journey became a separate entity, every bit as important as the destination.

Cindy felt as if she was flying, winging her way by the other racers. Before this, she barely would have noticed them. Certainly she wouldn't have recognized them as anything other than obstacles in her course. Today she saw the world through new eyes, people coming out for the thrill of the race, not merely the victory of the win. Mothers pushed infants in those fancy jogging strollers. Fathers bladed alongside their kids, faces alight with the simple joy of the day, of being here, part of the world.

She caught up and passed others who reminded her of the Cindy of old. Faces puckered in frowning concentration, oblivious to everything but the race, the upcoming curve, the next hill. And as she sailed by she felt somehow that Parker was with her. She could almost hear his voice ringing in her ears, coaching her when to pass, when to push herself, when to draft. And most of all, assuring her that, in his eyes, she was truly a winner.

The miles sped past in a blur. How could that be

when she could see things with a new and sudden clarity? Cindy laughed aloud at the absurdity of her own thoughts, then forced herself to concentrate anew on the race.

Confidence surged through her, lending new power to her limbs. She felt herself grin from ear to ear and didn't care how foolish she looked to the throngs of cheering onlookers as she headed into the final leg of the course.

Up ahead she saw the finish line marked by a slash of orange tape. The crowd's roar was drowned out by the rushing sound in her ears. She spotted Parker on the sidelines but didn't let the sight of him distract her as, with a burst of renewed determination, she recalled everything he'd taught her.

One final push propelled her forward. She felt the tape flutter across her chest. She heard the crowd roar and glanced around in a breathless daze. Did she do it? Did she cross the finish line first?

The judges stood off to the side in a huddle. Other skaters continued to power across the line amid cheering roars of congratulations. Where was Parker?

There he was. He and Marissa were bearing down on her and neither of them looked happy. When she heard the judges' ruling she realized why.

"You were robbed," exclaimed a vocal and belligerent Marissa as she reached Cindy's side. "I don't care what the judges ruled. Someone needs their eyes checked. I saw you cross the finish line and you were first. How dare they call it a tie?"

Cindy shrugged. "It was only a race." As she

turned to face Parker she felt her smile fade. What was wrong? Why didn't he pick her up and swing her around in his arms? Why wasn't anyone jumping up and down in excitement for her, clapping her on the back like that other girl's friends.

Had she let him down? Did her tie-finish of the race deem her a loser in his eyes?

He stood an arm's length away, his expression uncertain. "I'm sorry," he said. "I could have sworn you had it in the bag."

"It doesn't matter."

"You don't have to pretend to me. I know how important it was for you to win."

"No, really," Cindy said, frustrated that no one was listening to her. "I mean it. It doesn't matter. It was a great race."

"I'm going off to give those judges a piece of my mind." Marissa spun her wheelchair around sharply. "Someone must have it on video."

Cindy opened her mouth to try to stop her, then closed it again. She knew what her friend was like once she had her mind set a certain way. Marissa, intent in her role of mother lioness protecting her cub, was oblivious to the fact that Cindy didn't need protection.

She wanted to tell Parker she'd gained something far more valuable than any scholarship, but the words froze in her throat. It would only sound stupid and naive. Besides, why should he believe her? How could she possibly try to explain the metamorphosis she had just undergone? Something she didn't fully understand herself.

She stood shifting her weight from foot to foot. He was Parker. Familiar, and a stranger still. Or was he a stranger?

It wasn't that she felt whole when she was with him. She was complete on her own. Unlike that line in that Tom Cruise movie, "You complete me." She'd never felt one human being was capable of completing another. But they could complement each other. Support each other. Revere each other. The way Parker's parents did. The way Parker himself professed.

Impulsively she stepped forward and kissed him. "Thanks for cheering me on. You were an awesome coach."

He looked surprised. And no wonder. Usually he approached her, while she skittered away to her out-of-reach safety zone. He pulled her close. "Can we do that again?"

"Right after I shower. Don't you go away."

For once in her life she'd planned ahead, left a change of clothes along with toiletries and towel in a locker near the showers. For once she wanted to look her best for Parker.

When she emerged, showered and changed, he was standing relatively close to where she'd left him, his back to her. Her heart kicked into overdrive at the mere sight of him. The hemline of her long floral dress whispered across her calves, reminding her of her femininity. Perfectly complemented by Parker's masculine stance.

He turned just before she reached his side and the expression on his face made her *very* glad to be a woman. They faced each other for several long, silent moments. No words necessary, just a transfer of feelings and emotions that left Cindy feeling positively full to the bursting point.

"You look terrific," Parker said.

"Thanks." She took his arm. "Let's go get something to eat. I'm starved."

Party on the Green, Madronna Beach's annual summer solstice festival, was in full swing. Barbecues belched out savory smells of baron of beef and corn on the cob. Weavers, potters, sculptors, silversmiths and painters ringed the park's perimeter, stationed to demonstrate their crafts. Their presence added to the general melee as the plaintive melodies of jazz filled the air and competed with the excited chatter of hundreds of partygoers. In front of the bandstand stood a makeshift dance floor.

She turned impulsively to Parker. "Forget food. I'd rather dance." She kicked off her sandals and faced him barefoot, arms held toward him.

"What if I step on your toes?"

"Haven't you been doing that ever since we met? Or at least tried to?"

"Tried to what?"

"Step on my toes. Face it, you're used to organizing people. You like helping. You even buy your sister's shoes, for pity's sake."

"Too much White Knight?"

"Try for Prince Charming," Cindy said. "It'll get you further. A true prince knows how to dance."

"I have a bit of a block about dancing," Parker confessed. "The result of afternoons spent squiring some sweaty-palmed chubby ten-year-old around Miss Fensom's ballroom dancing classes."

*What a picture!* Cindy tried not to laugh, but in spite of her efforts a giggle escaped through her nose in the form of a snort. Once it was free, her laughter was unstoppable. She doubled over, arms clasped at her middle, laughter pouring out of her.

"It's not funny." Parker looked stern. "It was one of the definite low points of my adolescence. And I've never enjoyed dancing since."

Eventually Cindy got herself under control and tried to appear contrite as she stepped into his arms. "I predict I'm about to change the course of history," she said huskily, as she looped her arms around his neck. Parker was the perfect height for her to dance with, although he stood as wooden as a totem pole. "Relax. I'll even let you lead."

Parker cast her a glance tinged with suspicion. "What happened to you back there in the race?"

"Whatever do you mean?" She positioned her head comfily on his shoulder and reveled in the marvelous rightness of being in his arms. They found each other's rhythm as naturally as if they'd been doing it all their lives.

"You're different."

"Different how?"

"I'm not sure. It's something indefinable."

"I'm barefoot?"

"That's old news. Nope, I sense a change. Nothing visible to the naked eye. Just something I can feel."

Cindy drew back ever so slightly. He was right, of course. She had changed. A fact that was known to her and her alone, no matter what Parker felt or thought he felt. No one knew her well enough to be privy to such a personal thing. Not even her own mother. Despite what he might think or imagine, she and Parker weren't that close. His remark was only a lucky guess on his part. It had to be.

"Stop it." Her words came out sharper than she intended and she took a breath, forcing down the panic flaring through her. She strove to make her next words light and teasing. "You're starting to scare me. Making it sound as if I had some sort of epiphany out on the race course."

"Epiphany." Parker grabbed the word as if she'd tossed him a lifeline. "That's it exactly." He beamed at her, pulling her closer at the same time she tried to put distance between them. Mental distance.

They danced in silence for several minutes and Parker proved to be a much better dancer than he originally let on. What other secrets was he hiding?

"I thought you'd be bummed when you didn't come in first."

"Bummed. How could I be? That other woman and I get to split the scholarship money. And you know what? I talked to her before the race. She's a single mom with two kids who's never done anything like this before, either. On borrowed skates, no less. She trained for months.'' She pulled back and smiled. His eyes mirrored her reflection and Cindy realized she'd never seen herself look so happy. Never *felt* so happy ''The poor thing wasn't lucky enough to have you for a coach.''

''I didn't know you felt lucky. After all, I more or less forced myself on you.''

''Parker Davis. I thought I raised you better than that.''

It seemed quite deliberate, the way Parker's parents danced right into them and orchestrated a smooth exchange of partners.

''Nice race today, Cindy,'' Gord said. ''We were all proud of you.''

''Thank you, Dr. Davis.''

''So when's it going to be Dr. Stephens for you? Parker tells me vet school looms on your horizon.''

''I was hoping for this fall,'' she said. ''Depends on finances, of course.''

Gord Davis cleared his throat noisily. ''It's difficult, trying to do something like that all on your own, with no help.''

''Oh, I'll manage just fine.''

''I have no doubt.'' They danced stiffly in silence for several minutes longer. ''Those were difficult early years for Robin and myself. Didn't much take to being supported by my wife. Thought I ought to be able to do it all. You know what I mean. Learned it didn't make me weak, accepting help. Made me an all-around better person. And strengthened my marriage for all times.''

Cindy didn't know what to say. The music ended and he patted her awkwardly on one shoulder.

''I wish you the best of luck with it.''

''Thanks, Dr. Davis.'' After that they were set upon by Marissa and Tom.

Parker raised a brow at his old friend. ''Never expected to see you out on the dance floor.''

Tom beamed affectionately at Marissa. '''Mazing what a man'll do for a special lady.''

Marissa caught his hand in both of hers. ''And what that same lady will do for a special man.''

''Is that right?'' Parker asked as he swung Cindy away.

''I guess compromise comes into it someplace,'' Cindy said. ''Your dad was telling me pretty much the same thing.''

''Ah, the old give-and-take chat. Mom's famous for it, too. I think they own the copyright.''

Cindy laughed out loud.

Parker came to an abrupt halt. ''Have we danced enough? Can I buy you a baron instead?''

''You bet.''

They strolled arm in arm to the barbecue pit. Along with a baron of beef and iced tea, Parker insisted on buying Cindy a helium balloon with a picture of Goofy on in-line skates. She tied it to the shoulder strap of her dress and the balloon bobbed above them.

As they ate, they strolled around the park's perim-

eter, dodging easels and weaving looms, till Cindy
stopped short and swallowed thickly.

Parker stopped as well. "Something wrong?"

Cindy pointed. "It's Sheri. My mother."

Parker followed her gaze. "I saw her earlier,
watching the race."

"Really?" Cindy said. "That's an awful lot more
than anything she did when I was a kid."

"Maybe she's ready now to be a mother."

"You mean mature enough? Or simply suffering
misplaced pangs of guilt?"

"I mean ready."

Cindy gave him a long, searching look. "You do
come out with the darnedest observations, Parker Davis. Who knows? Maybe that makes two of us who
are ready." Dropping Parker's arm she started forward and surprised herself at the ease with which she
gave her mother a quick hug.

"Cindy." Sheri stood. "It's good to see you." As
her mother stood, Cindy noticed they were the same
height and build. There were other similarities as
well. She saw exactly what she'd look like in fifteen
years hence and felt relief. Her mother was beautiful,
but more than that she had an air of serenity about
her. A contentment Cindy longed to experience for
herself.

"Good to see you, too," Cindy said. "My friend
Parker said you were watching the race."

"Ah, yes, Parker. Such a nice young man."

Cindy felt her baron of beef, heavy in the pit of
her stomach. "I didn't know you knew Parker."

"He came out to the place." Sheri cocked her head to one side. "He said you were the one who told him about it."

"When was that?"

"I don't remember, exactly. Few weeks back." Sheri glanced from Cindy to where Parker was talking to another artist. "I figured the two of you had to be serious. For you to tell him about me."

"Why would you say that?" Cindy would have to be blind, deaf and dumb not to miss the hurt and vulnerable look on her mother's face. Suddenly she saw Sheri, not as a failure because she was different from other mothers, but as someone who loved her unconditionally. A mother who'd done the absolute best she could.

Cindy tried to picture herself right now with an eight-year-old child dependent upon her. The idea was more than a little scary. All her life she'd had only herself, her own needs and wants to deal with. Sheri had had the two of them. Cindy was suddenly so overwhelmed that words escaped her.

"I know I'm not the PTA mom you would have handpicked, Cindy. I know there were times I disappointed you. Times you were ashamed of me."

"Sheri." For the first time ever she saw the similarities not the differences between herself and the woman who'd given her life. "I was never ashamed of you."

Sheri pushed back a strand of hair that had pulled loose from her braid. "Times I was ashamed. Maybe it was my own guilt at not putting you up for adoption like everyone told me to. Not giving you at least a chance for that white-picket-fence type of family.''

"You're all the family I needed or wanted, Sheri. I am who I am today because of my—'' she smiled "—unorthodox upbringing.''

Sheri patted her awkwardly. "I've always been proud of you. I should have told you that more often, but the truth is you intimidated me. Right from the start you were stronger, brighter, smarter and more independent than I'll ever be. Ever could be.''

Cindy placed a hand on her mother's shoulder. "I'm proud of you, too, you know. You always believed in going for what felt right, no matter what anyone else said. I'm the same. And it's because of you.''

Sheri cleared her throat. "I'm just catching on to this mother stuff. Don't go making me a grandmother anytime soon, you hear?''

Cindy nodded. "I don't think you have any worries there.''

Sheri cocked her head. "I've seen the way Parker looks at you. The man has it bad.''

Cindy shrugged. "I'm way too young. I've no interest in getting serious about anyone. Not for a long, long time. There's too much other stuff I need to do first.''

"Such as?''

Impulsively Cindy found herself blurting out about vet school.

"That doesn't surprise me a bit. You were always tending to every stray and wounded creature that wandered near our place when you were young.'' She gave Cindy a long, warm hug. ''You'll do great. Promise you'll stop by for a visit when you get the chance.''

''I will. I promise.''

Parker felt a faint twinge of jealousy as he watched what had to be a reconciliation in the making between Cindy and her mom. He recognized the emotion even as he tried to squash it. It wasn't healthy to resent sharing Cindy with others. To want her all to himself. With a casual nod in Sheri's direction, he slung an arm around Cindy's shoulders.

''Ready to go?''

The look she sent his way was genuinely puzzled. ''Go where?''

''I thought we'd go celebrate.''

''Celebrate what?''

''Celebrate the day.'' Just then Parker's cell phone rang. Impatience clouded his face, to be replace by concern as he listened. ''Hang on, Con. I'll be right there.'' He passed Cindy a helpless look. ''Change of plans. Sorry.'' He grazed her forehead with a kiss and took off at a run.

CINDY REACHED FOR ANOTHER chunk of pizza in the cardboard take-out box. Across the table Marissa wiped her mouth with a paper napkin.

''You ought to be tucked up someplace having a romantic evening with Parker Davis. Instead you're here with me eating cold pizza and drinking warm Coke?''

"I thought that was the idea." She gnawed her lower lip. "I'm starting to look at Connie's interruptions as a blessing in disguise."

"How so?"

"The second I realized just how badly I wanted to be with him, I knew it was time to bail. My defenses seem to be crumbling. The man is getting to me."

"Your defenses are never weak," Marissa said knowingly.

"They are around Parker. He scares me, Rissa. It's like he sees right deep down to the core inside of me. Sees things no one ever sees."

"Because you don't let them." Marissa took a sip of Coke. "I'm hardly an expert," she said, "but it sounds to me as if the two of you are in love."

"Don't be silly. I have absolutely no intention of falling in love. Not for years and years, if ever."

"I don't think that's exactly how it works, hon."

"It is if I say so."

"Methinks the lady doth protest too much."

"Parker is..."

"Wonderful," Marissa supplied. "Handsome. Sexy. Thoughtful. Caring."

"Exactly. A real catch for someone who's in the market. I'm not."

Marissa crunched on her pizza for several long, thoughtful silent minutes. Cindy knew what that silence meant and steeled herself for Marissa's next words.

"Would you say I'm weak?"

"You?" Cindy scoffed. "You've got more

strength of character in your baby finger than most folks can wish for.''

"Exactly. But I need people. I need to be around them. Sometimes I need their assistance to do things I can't physically do on my own. I don't deny the need. And I also don't see it as a sign of weakness.''

"What's your point?''

"My point is, we're the same only different. I acknowledge my need. You don't.''

"That's because I don't. Need anyone, I mean.''

Marissa pressed her lips together in an expression Cindy knew well. It came up when they agreed to disagree.

Her friend heaved a big sigh, looked over at her and shook her head. "Girlfriend, I've never felt sorry for you before, but I do now. Plus, I think you're feeling a tiny bit jealous. That's the second time Parker's dropped everything and run to Conn.'' She said it casually, between strings of pizza cheese.

"Hey, the guy's a crusading white knight. And clearly some girl named Connie has first dibs.'' She forced a laugh. "At least it's not some girl named Tammy.''

Marissa almost dropped her pizza. "Did Parker never tell you who Conn is?''

Cindy stiffened. "No. And I never asked. Clearly it's none of my business.''

"Thank goodness Tom and I communicate better than the two of you. Just for the record, Conn is Parker's 'little brother.'''

"I thought he only had one sister.''

Marissa shook her head. "The other kind of 'little brother.' From what Tom said, the kid is going through some rough stuff. And Parker needs to learn to let go, not drop everything and run to the rescue."

As Cindy digested this latest information, she snuck a sideways glance at her best friend. Marissa was positively glowing.

"So you and Tom are communicating really well, are you?"

Marissa just continued to look smug. "You ought to give it a try. I recommend it."

# Chapter Thirteen

Cindy transferred the bottle of wine and fresh baguette to one hand and, with her free hand, reached for the knocker on Parker's front door. The sound echoed hollowly inside, but there was no answering movement. His truck and car were both in the nearby carport which, put together with the one tiny trickle of light around the side of the house, suggested he was home. She knocked again, louder this time, but not as loud as the noisy beat of her heart. This was such a huge risk for her, stepping toward someone rather than away from him. Risking rejection.

The door swung open on silent hinges, spearing the summer darkness with a blade of light. Parker stood before her looking definitely rumpled and not at all happy to be invaded.

"You busy?" Cindy asked with forced brightness in her tone.

"Kind of." His voice was muffled.

"Well then, I won't stay long." She took a step forward, followed by a second one, encouraged when he didn't slam the door in her face. "I picked up the new vintage from my favorite winery and couldn't think of anyone I'd rather share it with.''

He moved away from the door and she followed him through to the darkened living room. A few lights twinkled far out on the Pacific. Freighters, Cindy guessed.

"I'm afraid I'm not very good company." He clicked on one small sofa light, which shone down to the wood floor rather than up into their eyes. He flopped onto the couch with his legs splayed across the coffee table in front of him.

With far more confidence than she felt, Cindy made her way into the galley kitchen and rummaged through drawers and cupboards till she found a corkscrew and two wineglasses, along with a wooden board and a sharp knife.

"The way I see it, we never got to celebrate the other night after the race like we had planned." She paused in the doorway between the kitchen and the living room. "So here I am, bearing gifts. Well, sustenance, at least."

"So I see."

She set everything down next to him, opened the wine and poured them each a glass. Where normally she would have chosen a seat as far away from him as possible, she opted to pull a stool up close to where he sat.

His shirt was unbuttoned and he had at least two days' stubble darkening his chin. Clearly he was hurting, and Cindy just wanted to pull his head to her chest, to wrap her arms around him, to make the hurt go away.

She shrugged off the urge. Such actions weren't her style at all.

"I hope you don't mind. Marissa told me who Connor is. I thought you might want to talk."

Parker appeared to visibly attempt to pull himself together. He removed his legs from the table, sat up straight, ran a hand through his uncombed hair and reached for the glass of wine.

"This visit isn't one of those things you feel you owe me, is it? Debit-credit on the balance ledger."

Cindy shook her head and took a sip of wine. "But I have to admit, this is a new role for me. Usually I run from someone in need."

"And I never have before. So we're both taking on new roles."

"Learning lessons?" Cindy suggested.

Parker sighed heavily. "I thought I learned with Tammy. Some people don't want to be saved. Or even helped."

Cindy laid an encouraging hand on his bare arm and felt the tense flex of muscle beneath her fingertips. "Connor," she said softly. "Your little brother."

"Conn's sixteen now and out of the program. But I met him back when he was nine, spent time with him, letting him know someone out there cares."

"That's important."

"He got into trouble a while back and I bailed him out. The other night he got caught joy-riding in a stolen car. I realized he just expected I'd fix it again. Fix things the way I always had.''

''Instead you opted not to.''

Parker buried his head in his hands. ''Man, it was tough, turning my back and walking away. But he has to figure things out for himself. Even though I know it means his going into the system. And maybe getting in worse than he is already.''

''Or maybe learning something no one else can teach him. A tough lesson, but one he'll always remember.''

''I guess it's about fifty-fifty whether he sorts it out or not.''

She gave a small smile. ''Seems to me you like those odds. Besides, that's a better chance than he would have had without you in his life all those years.''

''Maybe.''

''Hey. If all these years you've been giving while he's been taking, that's a pretty imbalanced friendship.''

''He's not a bad kid. He's just confused.''

Cindy leaned close. She could smell Parker's California-sun-kissed skin, underscored with a musky male scent that did crazy things to her libido. ''Aren't we all?'' She leaned dangerously close. Close enough to kiss him. To taste the wine on his lips. His need of her. It was heady, being needed; no fear of her being the one in need. She wound her arms around his neck and hauled herself into his lap, loving this feeling of being needed. Of being close. Fears and insecurities evaporated as if they'd never existed.

Parker spoke against her lips as she took tiny nibbles of his mouth. "Just what do you think you're doing?"

"I thought if I plied you with wine and got you relaxed enough I might just manage to seduce you."

"Did you, now?"

"That was my intention."

"So you came over here with ulterior motives."

"I did, indeed."

"And you're not put off by finding me a mess."

"You mean not band-box perfect?" She ran a finger across the stubble darkening his jaw. "I like the stubble."

"Really?" He deliberately grazed her cheek with his unshaven chin. "I was just about to go shave."

"Don't you dare."

His mouth slanted across hers in hot urgency, a consuming desperation in his kiss. Cindy's blood sang in response as she tunneled her fingers deeper through his hair and reveled in the familiar comfort of being needed. Parker needed her.

She reclined back the length of the sofa, pulling him with her, his weight atop her an enticement as their limbs tangled and their breathing grew ragged. She allowed herself the freedom to explore the contours of his chest and back, thrilled to the feel of muscles bunching between her supersensitive fingertips.

Her lips replaced her hands, pressing fevered kisses

to his throat and the hair-spangled contours of his chest, his flat male nipples. She rubbed herself against him, regretting the soft denim of her shirt between his chest and hers. When he didn't unfasten the buttons fronting her shirt, she moved to do it herself. She needed to feel his hands, his lips upon her skin in return.

His hands atop hers stilled the movement. She couldn't quite comprehend it when Parker, gently, regretfully put her from him, inserting space between the two of them. She reached for him. Didn't he realize that she wanted him as much as he needed her?

She felt her old insecurities surface, slightly reassured by his words as he leaned down and pressed a light kiss to her forehead. "I need to have a shower first, Cinderella."

"Well hurry yourself and do that," Cindy said. "I'll meet you in the bedroom."

The second she heard the water start to run she peeled out of her clothing and tiptoed into the bathroom. She could just make out Parker's silhouette through the steam as she opened the shower door and slipped in next to him.

His face mirrored his surprise as he pulled her close. Cindy sank bonelessly into him.

"I think your arrival here has been one of the nicest surprises of my life."

"Here in the house or here in the shower?"

"Here, period."

He lathered the soap between his palms before gliding his wet, slick, slippery hands along the slope of her shoulders to that soft sensitive spot where neck and shoulder join, then around the nape of her neck, down her back, leaving a trail of overstimulated nerve endings in his wake. Cupping her buttocks, he angled her hips against his pelvis, leaving her no doubt as to his approval of her presence. Dreamily she rubbed against him, claiming the soap, drawing patterns in the whorls of chest hair, exploring the contours of well-honed pectorals, flat abdomen and narrow hips.

The pulsing shower spray beat a rhythm to match the wild staccato of her breathing mixed with his as he claimed her mouth for his own. She felt hot and wet and ravaged, inside and out, by the pounding spray, her pounding pulse, her clamoring senses. And Parker.

This evening had started out with him needing her; the balance had shifted to her need of him. Still, it remained a balance, she realized, where they needed and wanted each other equally. She gave herself over to his kiss, then arched back as he laved attention to her tightly swollen nipples, then slid his fingers through her slick folds to find that center point of all desire.

She shuddered with the sudden, unexpected force of her release, her cries of pleasure all but drowned out by the sound of running water. Her insides still pulsing with the aftermath of ecstasy, she tightened Parker's arms around her, wrapped her legs around his middle and guided him deep inside her. The tile wall was cool against her back, in contrast to the inferno stoked anew by Parker's possession of her.

Probing, stroking, pleasuring each other with their hands and lips and bodies, until the awareness of Parker's triumphant cry pushed her along with him to a new pinnacle of satisfaction.

Limp and spent, they regained their strength in each other's arms until Parker managed to reach back and turn off the water. The near silence, punctuated by the occasional drip of water and the ragged sound of their breathing was almost a surprise.

"Let me get you a towel," Parker said.

"Did you warm them in the dryer the way your mother does?"

He gave her naked behind a playful slap, then enfolded her in an oversize bath sheet. "This will have to do."

"It does fine."

She stepped out of the bathroom into the bedroom. "Any objections to me wearing your lucky shirt again?" As she spoke she opened the closet door and flicked on the light. Her breath caught in a shocked gasp. There, on a shelf, in its own brand-new shoe box was a red Louboutin pump. She watched herself almost in slow motion as she picked it up. Size eight, narrow. Right shoe only.

"Did you find the shirt?" Parker came up behind her and rested his chin on her bare shoulder. Pushing him away, Cindy turned and waved the shoe in his face. "Would you kindly be so good as to explain?"

A look she couldn't quite interpret crossed his face. Resignation? Guilt? Stubborn pride? Possibly a combination of all three.

"Believe it or not, the explanation is really pretty simple."

Nothing was *ever* simple. How had she managed to forget that? To allow her feelings for Parker to override her common sense.

"Why don't we both get dressed and you can tell me all about it," Cindy said. "Explain exactly how and why you lied and deceived me." She pushed past him to where she'd left her clothes in the middle of the floor and proceeded to get dressed.

"You refused to let me help you," Parker said as he stepped into his jeans and a clean shirt. "I didn't want to see you lose your job."

She faced him rigidly, fully clothed and back in control. Back to herself. "Where is the mate to this shoe? And more important, where did you get it from?" Her voice shook with the force of her emotions. She started to tremble and told herself it was righteous anger and indignation, not the pain of a breaking heart. Parker, on the other hand, looked calm and unruffled. She resented him that calm. How dare he?

"The mate, as I'm sure you already guessed, is the one I said I got from Hubble."

"So it's at the store."

"That's right. I bought an identical pair of shoes from someplace just outside of L.A. I don't remember the name of the store."

"Why would you do such a thing?"

"Hubble was gone, flown the coop with the real shoe. I knew how stressed you were about replacing it, so I thought I'd simplify your life a little. It was no big deal. Not nearly so big as you're trying to paint it.''

"No big deal? You don't think lying to me was a big deal?''

"I was wrong. I admit it. Okay, I made a mistake. At the time I was still on this crusade to save the world. Or at least the people in it who I care about.''

"You knew I wouldn't accept the shoe under those circumstances. No way, no how. Not even to save my job.''

"My intentions were honorable, Cindy. Even if my means to implement them were questionable.''

"Questionable? There's nothing questionable about what you did, Parker. And nothing further either of us has to say to each other.''

"WHAT DO YOU WANT ME to say, Park?''

"Remind me she's just too blasted much trouble. The whole female human race, for that matter. Except maybe Marissa. You two sure seem to have it licked.''

Tom ignored his blatant dig for information. "You never listened to me before. Why should I waste my breath now?''

"I thought you were my friend.''

"I am your friend. Precisely why I'm telling you to back off and leave the girl be.''

"What?'' Parker said sarcastically. "At the very least I expected to hear platitudes about how if you care about something, let it go. If it comes back it's yours and if it doesn't it never was.''

"Don't need me spouting that kind of drivel at you.''

"Cindy warned me right from the very start,'' Parker said moodily. "She said, never try and tame something wild.''

"I think you do that girl a disservice if you liken her to a wild creature. She seems pretty darn civilized to me. Just let her alone a spell. You can do that. You know you can.''

"If only she didn't find that darn shoe in my closet. I could have explained the whole incident when the time seemed right.''

"Would it ever have been right?''

Parker shrugged.

"Sooner or later she'd have caught on to you. Probably better having it sooner.''

"I really screwed up bad.''

"Give her some time. She knows you're not really such a bad guy.''

"Since when does living out here alone qualify you to be giving me advice about women?''

"You asked.'' Tom leaned back in his chair and scratched beneath his cap. "The human animal's not so different in many ways from the ones in the cages over there. To trust or not to trust. All comes down to an instinctual thing. So you'd best be asking yourself how can you rebuild her trust in you?''

"I haven't a clue. I had it once,'' Parker said, as he remembered a night with Chinese food and candlelight, when trust was a commodity both given and received. "I didn't realize at the time what a precious gift she'd given me."

"They say we often don't appreciate what we have till it's gone."

The words were spoken in a familiar female voice, and Parker did a double-take at the sight of Marissa wheeling herself toward them. "Marissa. I didn't know you were here."

She braked to a stop at Tom's side. "I knew you two needed some guy-talk time. I wasn't eavesdropping, really. I was out back working on my new painting. I just wondered if anyone else was hungry."

Tom jumped to his feet. "I'm sorry, sweetheart. I'll fix you something. Parker?"

Parker waved away the suggestion of food. He needed to see Cindy. To explain things to her. To make her listen this time.

Marissa shook her head, almost as if she could read his mind. "The worst thing you could do, Parker, would be to sit Cindy down and keep harping on this. Trust me. The absolute worst."

Parker exhaled heavily and tried to distract himself. "So you're painting up here? Walls or canvas?"

"Canvas," she said simply. "Tom fixed me up a studio out back and the light is incredible."

"So you two are serious?" He paused, frowned, clearly at a loss for words.

Her gaze met his, shadowed by a wisdom far beyond her years and her circumstances. "Say it, Parker. Whatever's on your mind."

He cleared his throat. "No offense, but you two seem to have a lot against a relationship working out between you."

"How so?"

"Tom lives up here, isolated from people. You don't drive. And this place wasn't exactly built with your needs in mind. Not like your place."

Marissa reached forward and laid her hand on his knee. "Those are simply physical obstacles, Parker. Nothing the two of us can't overcome. Certainly nothing insurmountable given the way we feel for each other."

He fell into gloomy silence. "You're right. Cindy despises me. That's way harder to overcome than a wheelchair ramp."

IT WAS BLISTERING HOT in the canyon, hillier than she recalled, and before long her legs were aching as she cycled to Tom's compound. She'd been surprised to hear Parker's buddy on the other end of the phone and even more surprised when he'd insisted on seeing her today.

Suspicious thoughts took over. A conspiracy. Parker had enlisted Tom's help to… To what? What could Tom do? Convince her to give Parker another chance? To accept his apology and move on. If that was his angle she'd set him straight right quick.

She needed to snap herself out of this blue funk she'd been in ever since last time she'd been at Parker's. It was over. Accept it, learn and move on. She sighed. She'd been a loner, comfortable and safe, for such a long time. Suddenly, it seemed, all these people had barged into her life. Parker's family. Maude. Sheri and Frank. Tom. Her phone had never rung so much as in the past few days. Why didn't everyone just leave her be? Let her hole up in peace?

She thought back to the Blade-a-Thon and tried to recapture the wonderful magical euphoria of the day. But the feeling eluded her, replaced by an overwhelming desire to flee.

From what was she running? From all those people? Or from Parker? The things he made her feel. She recalled riding with him, dancing with him, making love. Damn the man, for sweeping into her life and destroying all her carefully erected barriers. How had he done that? How had he scaled those safety walls she kept between herself and the rest of the world, only to betray her, to destroy the fragile bond between them. She had a gut feeling that the comfort zone she'd carved out for herself would never be the same.

At long last she reached Tom's compound, clambered from her bike on unsteady legs and collapsed beneath the shade of the one and only tree.

Tom must have been watching for her. He appeared seconds later, dragging a couple of folding chairs. Without a word he popped the top of a frosty bottle of beer and passed it her way.

Normally Cindy wasn't a beer drinker, but as she poured the icy liquid down her parched throat she had to admit she had never tasted anything quite so refreshing.

Tom seated himself next to her and raised his own beer bottle in a silent toast. ''Thanks for coming out on such short notice, Cin. It's nice having the company.''

Cindy wondered where Marissa was but didn't ask. Maybe Tom had asked her out here to talk about Marissa. She wiped her mouth with the back of her wrist and glanced around. ''I don't know. If I had a haven like this, I don't think I'd let anyone in here. Not ever.''

''Isolation's not all it's cracked up to be. A fellow can miss out on a lot.''

''You're not really isolated, though. You can come and go as you please, can't you?''

''Trouble with being alone all the time is social skills go into a decline. Before long you end up preferring your own company to that of most folks'.''

''You don't have an exclusive on that,'' Cindy said.

''Rumor has it man is a social creature. A clansman by nature.''

''Other people disappoint,'' Cindy said flatly.

''Not all. Not always,'' Tom said. ''It's natural to seek out a mate. Someone to laugh with.''

''Are you talking about you and Marissa?''

''Could be.''

In spite of herself, Cindy thought about Parker. He had a wonderful gift for making her laugh. Even their sparring was enjoyable.

''I prefer being alone,'' Cindy said stubbornly.

''Don't much blame you. Felt that way myself for

a good number of years. Convinced myself animals were far better company that humans.''

''You've got that right. They don't sneak around behind your back. They don't lie and deceive you.''

''They also don't encourage you to take a chance. Take a risk.''

Cindy twisted her hands in her lap. ''Something wrong with being safe?''

''Sometimes, by staying safe, a person manages to miss out on something a whole lot better. You know what I'm talking about.''

''Not really,'' Cindy said stubbornly.

''You had your doubts at first about me and your friend.''

Cindy relaxed. So that *was* what this little meeting was about. ''I was concerned at first. I didn't want to see Marissa get hurt. And then, I'll admit it, I felt a little bit displaced. She has you, she doesn't need me.''

''She still needs you, only different.'' Tom changed the subject. ''When do you start up at the animal hospital?''

''In the fall, I hope. I've already been accepted and paid my registration deposit.''

''Let me have a word. See about putting up a scholarship for the rest. You can intern with me if you have a mind to. I'm on the board, so it shouldn't be a problem.''

Cindy felt as if her eyes were about to pop out of her head. ''Are you serious? I'd adore the chance to do my field work with you. But I can't. I don't believe in borrowing money," she said flatly.

"Good policy," Tom said, pulling on his beer. "Generally speaking, it's my policy, too. But there are times when exceptions need to be made."

"Such as?"

"Medical emergency," Tom said. "If someone you cared about needed treatment, wouldn't you do whatever you needed to in order to raise the cash?"

"I suppose."

"What about following your dream?" Tom said. "You think this place just up and happened all by itself?"

"I don't know. Did it?"

"I had to kiss a lot of butts, smile and shake hands with a bunch of people I'd sooner avoid. But I swallowed my pride and made it happen. You can work in that shoe palace of yours come fall, or you can go to vet school the way you want. What's it to be?"

"I'll have to think about it," Cindy said.

"Offer's withdrawn then," Tom said, getting to his feet. "You don't want it bad enough."

Cindy jumped to her feet. "I do so!"

"Bad enough your gut burns and your teeth ache and some days you can hardly eat?"

Cindy flopped back down. He was describing the way she felt about Parker. And she didn't want to feel that way about another human being. Not ever.

Tom crouched next to her. "It's okay to accept a helping hand once in a while." He indicated the animals in his care. "Lotta those creatures wouldn't survive without human help right now. Doesn't make 'em any less than what they are. Creatures with strong survival instincts who know that refusing help means not to survive.''

"I'm so confused," Cindy said. "I hardly know what's what anymore."

"But you know who you are and what you want and where you're going."

"I thought I did. I'm not so sure anymore."

"I almost let go of this place, this dream, once," Tom said, squinting into the distance. "Almost listened to folks when they told me I ought to give up."

"How do you know?" Cindy said. "What's worth fighting for and what isn't?"

"Best I can figure," Tom said, "is when giving up means sawing a hunk of your soul off. You'll know."

As the afternoon wore into evening and Tom fetched more beer from the house, Cindy felt herself slip into a relaxed state of total mellowness as she lay back and stared up at the pink-streaked, darkening sky. She was floating, light-headed from the unaccustomed beer in her empty stomach, and enjoying the weightless sensation. Cindy sat up, tried to reach her feet and lost the struggle.

"Come on," Tom said. "Better get some food into you. It's not a good idea, drinking in this heat without having something to eat."

"Can't," Cindy said.

"Can't what?"

Cindy giggled. "Can't quite manage to catch my balance."

"How do you expect to ride that bicycle of yours home later?"

Tom bent down and scooped Cindy up in his arms. She wobbled and started to slip, grabbed onto the back of his shirt. He repositioned her more firmly. "How's that? Can you hang in there till we get to the house?"

"I'm just fine," Cindy said, but it was difficult enunciating her words clearly.

As Tom carried her across the compound, the night stillness was broken by the growl of a powerful truck engine. Seconds later headlights swept through the compound and blinded her in their glare.

The engine quit. The resultant silence sounded even more deafening, punctuated by the sound of a truck door being slammed. Cindy recognized Parker even before he appeared in front of them. His image swam in and out of focus before her.

"Come on in, Parker. Cindy and I have been having ourselves a little chat."

# *Chapter Fourteen*

"I don't want to chat with Parker, Tom," Cindy slurred against his shoulder. "I'm still mad at him." Her world spun and went black.

Parker shook his head at the sight of the limp rag doll in Tom's arms. "This is your idea of helping? Getting her drunk so she passes out?"

"How was I to know she isn't much of a drinker?" Tom said. "Here. Take her home and let her sleep it off."

"Why should I?" Parker said, but he took the limp form from Tom's arms and gazed on Cindy's slack but peaceful face, unable to resist holding her one last time, whether she was aware of it or not.

"You did her wrong," Tom said. "Expect it'll be up to you to put things right."

"While she's unable to argue, you mean," he said with a certain amount of irony.

"I get the feeling the lady'll always expect to have the last word. But I gave her some food for thought, at least."

"If she remembers any of it," Parker murmured.

At Cindy's apartment he fished the door key from her pocket and laid her gently down on her futon. She didn't even stir. He checked on her from time to time as he made a cup of tea, then settled down to wait.

Cindy awoke sometime before dawn with a dreadful pounding in her head and a mouth stuffed full of dry cotton. She moaned and rolled over, relieved to see she was in her own bedroom. She must have the flu. She felt dreadful. She squeezed her eyes shut, but the day before was a blur. She'd gone to Tom's. He'd given her an icy cold beer while they talked. She had a sense of something important having been said. What was it?

Eventually she got up in search of water. And tripped over a sleeping form on the floor. She yelped in surprise. The intruder stirred, muttered and sat up. Parker!

"What are you doing here?"

"Making sure you're okay."

"Why wouldn't I be okay?"

"We both know you're not much of a drinker. You were passed out cold."

"I'm fine now. I need to get ready for work." She took an unsteady step across Parker, wobbled and landed heavily on top of him.

"Oof!"

"You sleep on the floor, expect to get stepped on," Cindy said, scrambling to her feet.

"I figured I'd fare worse if you woke up and found me asleep next to you."

"The crusading white knight role is starting to wear awful thin."

"You're right. I even hung up my tattered cape a while back." Parker rolled to his feet. "Take an aspirin and drink lots of water. Oh, and eat something greasy. You'll feel better."

"I feel just fine."

He cocked her a glance. "Sure you do."

And then he was gone and Cindy was relieved. Wasn't she? Of course she was. Last thing she needed was Parker hanging around apologizing, explaining, trying to make up. Last thing in the world.

She slumped back down onto her futon and told herself she was glad he was gone. He wasn't to be trusted. How could she possibly be in love with someone she didn't trust?

CINDY SETTLED HERSELF cross-legged in front of the table, trusty calculator in hand, a sheaf of paper ready to record the logistics of her dream. She was going back to school this fall come hell or high water. Nothing would stand in her way. She didn't care if she studied all day and worked all night and never slept. She recalled Tom's generous offer, and even though she had no intention of accepting it, his belief in her ability helped fuel her determination.

Rummaging through the pile of papers in the middle of the table, she felt a fleeting moment of panic to discover her savings account book was missing. She'd had it at the Glass Slipper earlier today. She must have left it behind. She could get it tomorrow, but she was in the mood tonight for some serious number crunching. Besides, the exercise of the ride over would be good for her. Help chase away her muddled thoughts about Parker. Thoughts that were *not* fading with time.

As she rode down the street toward the shop she knew right away something was up, starting with the light being on inside of the store. Not the display light illuminating the front window, but the big glaring overhead fluorescent she rarely ever turned on during the day, even in December. But at this late hour the inside of the shop positively glowed like some nuclear space station, visible from blocks away.

She reached the shop, braked to a stop and dismounted almost in slow motion. The door was ajar. Through the window she could see Mr. Cheap inside, gesturing theatrically to a man whose back was toward Cindy. Could it be a robbery in progress? She tried to catch Mr. Cheap's eye, to see if she ought to run for help, but when his glance lit on her he beckoned her inside.

Hesitantly she pushed the door open wide and stepped into the surreal fluorescent glare. As she approached the cash desk, the other man spun around.

Cindy gulped. Mr. Hubble. And reposing innocently on the cash desk between the two men was a red Louboutin pump.

Mr. Cheap gestured at the shoe in an agitated manner. "Mindy," he said, still unable to get her name straight. "Hubble here has just returned some very baffling merchandise to me. This shoe, which he claims to have found outside of the shop one night, lying on the road.''

"Oh,'' Cindy said.

"Oh, indeed. Very baffling. Especially considering that when I check our inventory control figures I see we only ever had one pair of eight, narrow. A pair that is happily resting inside their box, right where they're supposed to be.''

In spite of herself, Cindy was impressed. She'd had no idea Mr. Cheap knew how to turn on the computer, let alone locate a pair of shoes from their massive storeroom.

"Hubble here claims you made contact with him regarding the found shoe. Care to explain to me, the lowly shop owner, just what in the Sam Hill is going on?''

Cindy's mind drew a blank. What could she say? What possible explanation would bear scrutiny? "Well, sure I...''

"Because I can't have an employee I can't trust. No one pulls a fast one on Cecconni. Not the Big C.''

Cindy bit back a smile upon hearing the short, balding man refer to himself as the Big C. "It's a simple explanation, Mr. C. The shoe belongs to a friend of mine and she'll be really glad to get it back.'' Cindy reached for the Louboutin.

"Not so fast!'' Mr. Cheap swatted her hand like one might swat a pesky mosquito. "Hubble wants to see the shoe returned to its rightful owner, don't you, Hubble?''

Mr. Hubble nodded, his Adam's apple bobbing in his chicken neck in time to his actions.

"No problem," Cindy said. "Just let me make a quick call."

She reached for the phone and dialed Marissa's number, passing the two men a forced smile as she counted the rings at the other end.

"Hello?" A sleepy-sounding man's voice left Cindy temporarily tongue-tied. "Hello?"

"Sorry," Cindy said. "I must have the wrong—"

"Cindy? It's Tom. You looking for Marissa? She's in the bath."

*In the bath?* She'd suspected things between Tom and her friend had progressed far beyond friendship. Obviously she'd been right.

"Tom. I'm over at the shop. I need to have Marissa join me here and bring the other red Louboutin pump. It's at Parker's house. Do you understand? I need her to get here with it as quickly as possible."

"Cindy, you sound funny. Is everything okay?"

"It's a bit difficult to explain right now. But everything will be fine once Marissa shows up with that other shoe."

"Okay then. I'll tell her." She heard the puzzled hesitation in Tom's voice, and it stayed with her as she hung up.

"See?" Cindy turned brightly to the two men. "This'll all get sorted out in a minute."

"I can't wait," Mr. Cheap said with heavy sarcasm, as he folded his arms over his chest. "Because, looking at someone's bank book that I found here—"

he produced Cindy's missing passbook "—I was starting to wonder if someone was pulling a fast one on the Big C."

Cindy eyed the missing bankbook and licked her lips nervously. She didn't care for the way things were playing out right now. Not in the least. Her plan's success hinged upon her working all summer. But Mr. C. wasn't smiling as his eyes met hers.

"Why didn't your friend buy her shoes from here, Mindy? That's a pretty big sale we missed out on. Three bills, right? Makes a boss wonder at the loyalty of his staff."

"I'm not really sure."

The clock ticked loudly, each minute seeming to stretch into an hour, when suddenly pandemonium broke out in the shop as people spilled through the open door. Besides Marissa and Tom, there were Parker and his parents, along with Cindy's mother and Frank. Then Hilary ambled in with her boyfriend, and Maude from next door to Hubble squeezed in near the cash desk. Melody Manners must have smelled a scoop, because she was also in attendance at what was starting to resemble something from a zany *I Love Lucy* rerun. Cindy felt as if half of Madronna Beach was jammed inside the shop, and everyone was talking at once. Sheri and Maude started to jabber with Parker's parents.

"Silence!" Mr. C. roared, standing on a stool in order to be taller than anyone else. Everyone stopped talking and turned to stare. "I smell a conspiracy."

He pointed. "You there in the wheelchair. Let's see if the shoe really does fit."

Picking up the trouble-causing pump, Tom knelt and slipped the shoe onto Marissa's slender foot. Cheap was still unimpressed. "No offense, girlie, but what do you need fancy footwear for?"

Marissa smiled. "A good investment. They never wear out?"

Hubble clasped his hands together, a tear in his rheumy old eyes. Maude trundled next to him and gave his hands a squeeze. "This girl's already spoken for, my dear."

He nodded, his Adam's apple bobbing.

"So where the heck's the other shoe?"

"I've got the mate." Parker stepped forward. "I've also got something else to say, and now seems as good a time as any." His gaze captured Cindy's as he stepped forward, the shoe balanced on the palm of his right hand. She had never seen Parker look less sure of himself. In fact, judging from the intensity of his gaze on hers, they could have been the only two people in the room. Or on the planet.

"Wait a minute. How come you have the shoe?" Cheap narrowed his eyes.

Parker's gaze never left Cindy. "Believe it or not, it's the shoe's mate that ultimately led me to my mate." He passed the shoe to Cindy and she took it, noticing right away it was off balance. Toe-heavy.

"What's in the toe?"

Parker stuffed his hands in his jeans pockets. "Take a look and see."

"I'm not sure I want to."

"Still afraid of taking those risks? Then you're not the person I think you are." His words were the challenge he knew they would be. A subtle murmur ran through the crowd, urging her on.

Cindy took a breath, fished around the toe of the shoe, and brought out a small round jeweler's ring box. Those gathered fell silent, almost in time. Everyone shuffled closer, their attention focused solely on her.

She glanced in Parker's direction. If possible, he appeared even less sure of himself than before.

"Parker?"

"Wait," he said. "Hear me out. You trusted me once before. And maybe I don't deserve a second chance, but I'm asking for your trust again. Right now my biggest fear ever is that you'll reject me in front of all these people. But I'm facing that fear head-on. Taking a chance. I need you and want you in my life, forever, Cinderella. I know we won't always see eye to eye. I know you don't want my help with your schooling. But look at my parents. They made it. I want us to make it. And I promise, in front of everyone here, that I'll never pull anything on you ever again, the way I did with the shoe. Not even if I truly believe, from the bottom of my heart, that it's for your own stubborn good. Please give me the chance, Cinderella. To prove I'm worthy of your love and deserving of your trust."

Cindy opened the ring box. Nested inside on the burgundy velvet was the most exquisite ring Cindy had ever seen, a solitaire diamond winking in a pumpkin-shaped cut. The crowd oohed and aahed. Cindy looked from the ring to the people gathered around. Parker's mother smiled confidently. Her own mother gave an encouraging nod.

"Marry me, Cindy. And let's learn the rest of life's lessons together."

She felt the old familiar panic, her fear of needing someone as much as life itself. Then miraculously it dissipated, like fog burned off by the sun's warming rays.

Parker had made himself vulnerable, surmounted his own fear. It was time now for her to do the same. She extended her left hand, relieved to see it didn't tremble. Parker freed the ring from its bed and slipped it onto her finger. Everyone started to applaud.

Cindy passed Hubble the other shoe. The spotlight shifted from her to Marissa as Hubble knelt, a smile transforming his lined and weathered face, as he slid the matching shoe onto Marissa's bare foot. No one voiced an objection when Melody captured the moment on film.

Cindy slid her hand inside of Parker's. She hoped he knew that her move signaled her trust and her love. "I wish we were alone." She mouthed the words.

"Soon," Parker promised, drawing her snug against his side. The weight of his arm was a comfort, not a restraint, and Cindy leaned into him, aware that the assembled guests were beaming at him. Her mother came up and congratulated them both. Parker introduced his parents to Sheri and Frank and the two mothers immediately started to talk weddings.

Mr. Cheap, meanwhile, focused on Marissa. "Hey, aren't you that artist?"

Marissa beamed. "I'm a fabulous artist."

"My set designer at the theater is leaving. You need a new challenge, you come see me."

"I will." Marissa smiled up at Tom. "As soon as we get back from our honeymoon."

More congratulations flew around the room, adding further fuel to the noise and excitement. Mr. Cheap rose to the occasion, pulling out some champagne from his office refrigerator and toasting the happy couples, offering a twenty percent discount to anyone who made a purchase that night. Cindy smiled as she saw Maude fondling a fussy pair of fuchsia-colored sandals.

When Parker finally pulled her into his arms and sealed his promise of their future with a very thorough kiss, no one seemed to notice or to care. The Glass Slipper rocked with laughter and well-wishes, while out in the town square, the clock struck twelve.

Parker and Cindy both heard it. "Midnight," Parker said. "You're not going to run off on me, are you? Barefoot and all."

"Not a chance," Cindy said. "I have everything I need right here. For now and for always." She paused to admire the wink of her diamond solitaire in the light. "My pumpkin and my Prince."

# *Epilogue*

Dr. and Mrs. Gordon Davis are delighted to announce the marriage of their son, Parker Davis, to Dr. Cindy Stephens. The couple were joined in a private ceremony in Bermuda, where the bride was attended by her mother, Ms. Sheri Stephens, and her best friend, Mrs. Marissa Wilson. The happy couple plan to make their home in Madronna Beach.

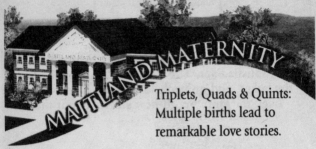

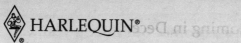